Smile

To Sara

Suzanne Craig-Whytock

*Love
Aunt Suzanne*

BookLand
press

Published by BookLand Press
15 Allstate Parkway
Suite 600
Markham, Ontario L3R 5B4
www.booklandpress.com

Printed in Canada

Front cover image © Cherriesjd

Library and Archives Canada Cataloguing in Publication

Craig-Whytock, Suzanne, author
     Smile / Suzanne Craig-Whytock.

Issued in print and electronic formats.
ISBN 978-1-77231-065-8 (softcover).--ISBN 978-1-77231-066-5
(EPUB).--ISBN 978-1-77231-067-2 (PDF)

     I. Title.

PS8605.R3467S65 2017   jC813'.6   C2017-903076-0
                                                C2017-903077-9

We acknowledge the support of the Canada Council for the Arts, which last year invested $153 million to bring the arts to Canadians throughout the country. We acknowledge the support of the Ontario Arts Council (OAC), an agency of the Government of Ontario. We acknowledge the financial support of the Ontario Media Development Corporation for our publishing activities.

Chapter 1

When I was a little girl, my parents bought me a sandbox. It was bright blue with yellow trim, and it had those corner benches you could sit on while you were playing. I was never that dainty; I'd get right in there with my Care Bears shovel and pail, and dig for hours. Dad used to joke that I'd end up in another country one day; I used to fantasize about digging a tunnel and coming out the other end into a wonderful land where everything was upside down and in technicolour, the people wearing big, wide hats and vibrant costumes, speaking in a strange language that only I could understand. There's a picture of me playing in that sandbox—Mom keeps it in a silver frame in her bedroom. I'm looking up at the camera, curly dark hair, rosy cheeks, and a huge grin on my face. I'm surrounded by piles of sand, and I'm waving my shovel. Dad's sitting on one of those little corner benches, leaning forward behind me and making a silly face. It's a perfect scene of a picture-perfect child and a loving father. Everyone still has that picture of me in their heads. It looks like this: Cassandra Wilson, sweet 16 going on 17, the self-possessed quiet girl who has it all together and knows exactly where she's going. At least that's what everyone else sees. But when I look in the mirror, I have no idea who's looking back. The voice inside my head doesn't always match up to what I see in the mirror. The smile on my face has become an easy way to avoid dealing with questions and concerns. And I don't dream about perfect fantasy lands anymore—I learned a long time ago that they don't exist.

◆ ◆ ◆

On Wednesday morning, I have an appointment at the guidance office. Mr. Pratt is a stickman with big pop-out eyes—he seems perpetually surprised to see you, like he didn't expect you to keep your appointment. He has three ties and three shirts which he wears in different combinations—blue tie with green striped shirt, brown tie with red checked shirt, green tie with blue shirt, and so on. All his ties are the same woven material and they're all too long, so he tucks them into his pants. As far as guidance counsellors go, he's a bit scatterbrained—for example, not telling you that you need a specific math course to graduate until halfway through the semester. But on his plus side, if you want to call it that, he actually does care about his students. I heard that once he stayed all night at the hospital with a suicidal grade nine girl because he wanted to support her and her parents. Now that's dedication for you. Of course, he's not really as perceptive as he thinks—like everyone else, he just sees the face I put on for the world. Which explains our little meeting this morning.

"Well, Cass," he starts.

"Hi, Mr. Pratt," I smile with fake cheer. "Your plants look wonderful."

He grins back, then reaches into his desk and pulls out a little bottle of Amazing-Grow plant fertilizer.

"I took your advice," he whispers, looking around as if garden spies are everywhere, "and it really worked.

Thanks for the tip!!" He hides the bottle back in the desk drawer. I smile cheerfully again and wait as he begins to chatter on about his plants. Mr. Pratt's office is dimly lit at this time of the morning (although he gets the "mid-day sun", as he likes to tell everyone), and the dust motes are dancing in the weak light. I find this fascinating; as I watch them, I think about ballet. I took ballet lessons for years. I really loved dancing—I would never have been a super-star, but I was good enough to make my Dad proud of me. He took me to every practice, came to every recital, got us tickets to see The Nutcracker when I was 6, and made me promise to keep dancing even after... well, unfortunately, it was expensive, and I realized as I got older that there was no point in making Mom pay for lessons with money we didn't have if I wasn't going to be a professional dancer. She said it didn't matter, that she'd keep paying for classes, but it wasn't fun anymore, and I felt so guilty. I finally begged off when I announced that I wanted to pursue archaeology as a career—too much studying; therefore not enough time for twirling. It made my mother sad—she's always been a little uncoordinated, and loved that I wasn't—but I think she was relieved at the same time. I miss it, but we all have to make sacrifices, right?

"...university?" Mr. Pratt was saying.

"Maybe you could recommend the best ones for my program," I answer, taking a guess at where we are in our conversation. Lucky again. Mr. Pratt continues,

"Well, I've been doing a little research for you—I hope you don't mind—"

I smile brightly and murmur something like, "Oh no, of course not, thanks."

"I discovered—it's very interesting—that the top three schools for archaeology are..."

Blah, blah, blah. And so it goes.

I walk into English class 10 minutes late, thanks to my guidance appointment. Mr. Pratt likes to be thorough. I give my permission slip to Mrs. Gilman to check, which she does without missing a beat in whatever she's saying to the class. It's probably about some poem — we've been doing poetry for what seems like forever at this point. Mrs. Gilman loves poetry, I mean really reveres it. When she talks about a poem, she gets all breathless and inarticulate, as if she's so overcome with passion that she can't think straight. I used to like poetry a long time ago. I wrote a couple of decent poems when I was in Grade 9, but I made the mistake of handing one to Mr. Jacobs, my English teacher that year. I wrote a note at the bottom that said, "Please don't read this to anyone." I even put a happy face next to the note, an extra bit of sugar. Two days later, he pulls my poem from the top of his stack, reads it to the whole class and says "Can you believe Cass didn't want me to share this wonderful poem with anyone?!" I just smiled and looked at my desk, secretly horrified. Well, that's what I get for sharing. I sit down at my desk now and open my books. Across the aisle, Tara Connelly and Megan Pearson are writing notes back and forth, and snickering softly. Megan points to the front corner of the room, then turns and giggles at Tara again. I look. Danny Stryker is sliding into the front corner desk, late as usual. His hair is green today, and shaved into a mohawk. He hears Megan and Tara, and turns around casually, looking with a bemused expression at the room in general, then faces front again. It's strange — I don't ever think I've heard him speak.

Mrs. Gilman's room is a sensory overload — posters everywhere with inspirational messages like "Hang in There", and "Teamwork Gets the Job Done!", pictures of cars and kittens, student work carefully mounted on coloured Bristol board, a live goldfish in a tank in one corner, plants everywhere. What's with the teachers here and plants, anyway? I focus on Mrs. Gilman. She's saying "And what Thomas meant when he said 'Rage, rage against the dying of the light' was that he wanted his father to fight death, to struggle against it, to not succumb gently to the inevitable. You see? It's a very personal piece; you can only imagine how difficult it would be for anyone to lose a father they loved so much..." She stops for a brief second, barely noticeable, and makes a point of not looking at me before she starts talking about the imagery in the second stanza. I smile into the space in front of my desk. My father died of cancer when I was ten. I don't like to talk about it. When I think about it, it just reminds me of the empty space inside me where he's supposed to be, so I try not to think about that either. At the funeral, everyone kept saying how sorry they were until I wanted to punch someone in the face. I didn't though. I stopped crying and just started to smile, this perfect, serene smile. When I saw the hole that they dug for his casket, I smiled even harder.

♦ ♦ ♦

Despite the fact that there are only 20 minutes left before the final bell, I have an overwhelming need to go to the bathroom. Not to pee — I just need desperately to get out of French class. If I have to conjugate another verb, I'll gouge my own eyes out. When I ask Mademoiselle Boisvert, she narrows her eyes at me and says, "Bien sur," in a gruff voice. Mlle Boisvert is scary — heavyset, with hair like a wire brush, close-cropped at the sides and a little longer on top, military style. She likes polyester pantsuits and doesn't wear any jewellery except for a silver whistle that hangs on a chain around her neck. When the class is getting too loud, she blows her whistle at us, alternating that with "Attention!" Definitely very military, if you know what I mean. She has a partner named Patty — there are pictures of the two of them stuck on Boisvert's filing cabinet from their vacations together — hiking on the Bruce trail, whale watching off Newfoundland, stuff like that. It looks like they're having a good time in all the pictures. It's weird to think of teachers having normal lives outside of their classrooms, with houses, and families that love them. It's sweet in a way, considering Boisvert hardly ever looks that happy at school.

I walk to the bathroom, hoping for a little peace and quiet. Not a chance. I'm not in there for 30 seconds, when the door swings open again and Missy Goldman and Suneeta Darwali launch in, shrieking with laughter.

"Oh my God!!" says Missy.

"Oh my God!!" says Suneeta.

Obviously, they are both amazing conversationalists. When they finally stop grabbing each other and exploding into fits of giggles and more Oh my Gods, they realize I'm standing there.

"Oh my God, Cass!" says Missy. "You'll never believe what just happened!"

"Mr. Aikens was doing this thing," Suneeta blurts out, "and Tommy Fillmore turned on the Bunsen burner and lit up this piece of paper—"

"—Mr. Aiken just about got his ass set on fire!" They both finish in screeching unison, collapsing into a hysterical heap again.

I smile. "That sounds really crazy. What's going to happen to Tommy?"

Suneeta snorts. "Nothing, of course. You know Tommy—Aiken sent him to the office, and he gave Mr. Verde some story about how it was an accident. He just got sent home for the rest of the day."

Missy walks over to the sink next to me and peers into the mirror. Her eyeliner is running from laughing too hard. She looks sideways at me and says, "No Tommy for the rest of the day. Too bad, huh, Cass?"

"Too bad for Tommy," I laugh, opening my purse and rummaging for a hairbrush. When are these two idiots going to leave me alone?

"I heard from Steve Franklin that Tommy thinks you're hot," Missy continues in a teasing voice, still trying to wipe off the raccoon circles under her eyes.

"Yeah?" I reply. I'm trying to sound vaguely interested in that coy, "he couldn't possibly mean me" way. Actually I couldn't care less. Tommy's an absolute moron and I'm annoyed that he's been discussing me with the rest of his jock friends. I keep smiling and brushing my hair.

"God, you've got great hair," says Suneeta. "I'm so-o jealous. I can't do anything with mine unless I use a gallon of product, it's so straight."

"Hey, Cass," Missy interrupts, "I overheard Ms. Jackman and Mr. Pratt talking about you wanting to be an archaeologist. Is that true?"

"Yeah," I say, putting the hairbrush back in my bag.

Suneeta leans against the tile wall, hands in pockets, looking up at the ceiling dreamily. "Archaeology is soooo cool. All those gorgeous tanned guys digging up dinosaur bones."

Missy laughs. I say, "No, actually that's palaeontology. It's different."

They both look at me with admiration. I smile back. Missy says "Don't you have French right now? How'd you get Boisvert to let you out?"

"I had to go," I reply. It's the truth.

Suneeta laughs, "Well, when you gotta go..." and they both turn to leave.

"Bye, Cass!"

"See you!"

"See you later," I say to their retreating backs.

The door swings shut. I'm left in silence again, blissful silence. I turn back to the sink and run my wrists under the cold water for a minute, then dry off and get back to class before the bell rings.

This whole archaeology thing is really snowballing out of control. It started off as a private joke — after I quit ballet, I got sick of people constantly asking me what I wanted to do instead when I finished high school so I picked something cool, something that every six-year-old wants to be.

It never occurred to me that people would take it seriously. Then my Mom started buying me books, and Mr. Pratt
started "researching" it for me—why didn't I say engineer-
ing? That's nice and vague—no one knows what they really
do anyway. The truth is, I don't want to do anything after
high school—I have no plans whatsoever. Maybe I'll run
away and join the circus—it couldn't be any worse than archaeology.

◆ ◆ ◆

I live about six blocks away from school, so the walk home
is short—established family neighbourhoods with mature
trees—a real estate agent's dream. I move at a leisurely
pace—the sun is dappling the leaves on the trees, and I
breathe in the scent of lilacs and newly-mown grass. Dad
used to mow our lawn every Saturday morning. I loved sitting on the top porch step, the sound of the lawn mower
a faint hum, getting louder and louder, until he appeared
around the corner of the house huffing and sweating. As
soon as he saw me, he'd always smile and give me a mock
salute. When he finished making those perfect green stripes
he loved so much, he'd go into the house, and come back
out with two glasses of lemonade. We'd sit and drink, the
ice cubes clinking against the perfection of the quiet, sun-
drenched morning. He'd put his arm around me and I'd
lean into him, his T-shirt smelling of fresh grass. But that
was a long time ago; my mother gets one of the neighbourhood kids to do the grass now.

My house is on the corner, a huge Victorian mon-
ster with wraparound porches and a turret. It's a great
house really—it was in my Dad's family for generations,
and it was built by his great-great-grandparents. His great-
great grandfather was some kind of flaxseed tycoon, one
of our small town's founders. He came from Scotland, and
built a huge mill at the end of town, as well as this house.
My mother just lives for the place—she's into antiques and

town heritage in a big way. I like our house actually, even though it's getting pretty run-down—it has a lot of quiet spaces, rooms full of silence and solitude, smelling of lemon oil and old wood. It's much too big for just the three of us, and it costs a lot to upkeep, but after Dad died, Mom announced that she would never sell it, no matter what it took, and she's been working overtime ever since just to barely maintain it. I guess she had too many good memories to ever let it go. I'm glad though, despite the cost. I feel close to Dad in a weird way when I'm here, like he's not actually gone, but just in another room.

I have about ten minutes to enjoy it before my little brother gets home. He's nine—he was around three years old when my dad died, and he doesn't remember him at all. Like most little brothers, Chris can be extremely annoying, but I love him and he makes me laugh my butt off—he's currently obsessed with some cartoon character called "The Almighty Rat". The Almighty Rat is just that—a great big RatMan who fights crime from his crumbling old tenement headquarters. Chris has taken to talking in this weird Ratvoice lately. For example, if you ask him to help with the dishes, he'll say, in a crazy high-pitched, voice, "Ah, Almighty Rat no do dishes. Must battle vermin of the universe." The worst thing (or the best, according to Chris) is that the lunatics who created the Almighty Rat have recently embarked on a merchandising extravaganza and came out with Rat costumes just in time for Chris's birthday. Of course, Mom got him one, and he wears it all the time. It's like orange pyjama bottoms, a royal blue, long-sleeved top with a great big rat on the front, and a yellow cape that ties at the neck. He looks insane when he wears it, which is usually 30 seconds after he gets home. Mom told him that he wasn't allowed to wear it to school though, for which I'm eternally grateful.

When Chris finally bursts in, throwing his backpack against the wall by the front door, he's completely hyped for another afternoon of the Almighty Rat, this time with a friend, some shady-looking kid named Nolan. All I get in the rush is "Hey Cass! Nolan... out back... karate... Almighty Rat suit?!!! I point to the laundry basket at the top of the basement stairs. He grabs his costume and flies out the back door. Nolan follows more slowly.

"Got anything to eat?" he asks, scanning the kitchen with doubtful eyes.

"I think there're cookies in the cupboard," I answer. "Want some?"

He contemplates this for a moment. "Sure," he says finally.

I hand him the bag. "Knock yourself out, Nolan. Make sure Chris gets some."

"Right" he says, hand already in the bag, and disappears out the back door.

After a few minutes, I look out the kitchen window—Nolan is spitting cookie crumbs at Chris, who's warding them off with Rat-style karate chops and kicks. I feel vaguely guilty, like I should say something, but Chris looks like he's having fun, so I don't. It would be nice for Chris to have a friend to hang around with. Not that there's anything wrong with him exactly, but he was born really prematurely, over a month too early, and he has some problems. Nothing super-noticeable—his lungs were underdeveloped and he still has breathing problems, but the main thing is, if you spend enough time with him, you realize that he seems really young for his age. Thoughtless people might call him "slow", but I call him "unique". He has this ability to see the world as the most amazing place, which is great, but he's also really gullible and he'll believe anything you tell him, which makes him a target sometimes for jerks. I hope Nolan isn't one of them. I'll make sure to keep an eye on them. I always keep a good eye on Chris, no matter how annoying he can be.

Before dinner, I watch Chris and Nolan for a few more minutes—things seems to be going well despite the crumb-spitting and karate-chopping—then I turn to the task at hand—what to make for dinner? I open the freezer and stare at the contents, then spy a frozen lasagna. I pull it out and grab a head of lettuce and a couple of tomatoes from the refrigerator. Lasagna and salad—sounds fine to me. I'm mostly responsible for preparing meals because Mom leaves the house before 7:30 am and doesn't get home until way after 6:30 pm. She's an insurance adjuster, which means she spends a lot of time telling people whether her company will pay up when their basement floods, roof leaks, porch falls off, barn falls down—all those natural disasters that seem to happen to her clients on a fairly regular basis. Before Dad died, Mom stayed at home. She had a part-time job in a second-hand clothing store downtown that her friend Charlotte owned, but she was always here when I left for school and when I got home. She really loved working at Charlotte's, but then we needed more money, so she got a full-time job as a secretary with Provincial Life and went to night school to work her way up. Our paths don't cross much anymore. She works a lot of overtime to make extra money to pay all the bills. We used to be pretty close, but now she's hardly ever here, and when she is, I'm either doing homework, or working myself.

I work in this weird clothing store called You Jane. The owner got the name from the old Tarzan movie, where Tarzan's big line was "Me Tarzan, you Jane?" I don't know what it has to do with clothes. We don't sell any animal prints or bathing suits, but the store's all decorated in this ridiculous jungle theme with vines hanging all over the place and jungle beasts painted in murals on the walls. The clothes we sell aren't bad—I get a discount so at least half my wardrobe is from You Jane—and a lot of the girls I know all shop there too, since it's in the mall. Most of the time, it's ok, but every once in a while, someone comes in and acts completely bizarre. For example, I had a guy come in last week, and when I asked if he needed any help, there was a big long pause during which he just stared at me.

"Do you need help with anything, Sir?" I repeat.

"Yes,' he says, still staring. That's it—just yes.

"OK then," I smile, feeling like I'm talking to a five-year-old "What can I help you with?"

"I need a shirt," he answers. OK, now we're getting somewhere.

"Great!!!" I say enthusiastically. Well, we carry a lot of different kinds of shirts. What style are you looking for?"

"I don't know." He starts staring at me again. Back to square one. After another long pause, him still staring and me smiling ferociously, he suddenly blurts out, "I want something in in-dee--go." He pronounces each syllable of indigo separately and it takes me a minute to register what he means.

"Oh, indigo blue," I reply cheerfully. I look around and realize we have nothing in indigo.

"Wow," I say, my voice full of mock regret. "I'm really sorry, but we don't have anything in that colour this season. I'm pretty sure though that I saw some indigo shirts in Sears a couple of days ago. That's just down the other end of the mall." I smile again, hoping beyond all reason that this guy will just go away. He stares at me again.

"No—," he starts.

"Sears!!!" I finish firmly. "Well, thanks for coming in, though!" And with that, he wanders out of the store looking vaguely lost. I hope he made it to Sears, but I have my doubts. Yeah, my job is very intellectually challenging. Well, what do you expect for minimum wage? I don't have a lot of choice anyway—with just Mom working, money was pretty tight, so as soon as I was old enough to get a job, I've been doing whatever I can to help out the family. I figure, if Mom has to work overtime to put food on the table, the least I can do is contribute. We have a system—Mom works late 3 nights a week and I look after Chris, and I work after school the other two nights (and every Saturday) and he goes to the neighbour's house until Mom gets home. I've had to give up after school activities, and I don't have much of a social life, but I know Mom appreciates it.

I hear my mom's car pull into the driveway. I watch from the front window as she gets out, goes to the passenger side, and takes out her briefcase and some file folders. She looks tired. When she comes in, I've got the salad ready and I'm in the process of setting the table.

"Hi, sweetie," she says, dumping her briefcase on the floor and depositing the folders on the counter.

"Hi, Mom. Dinner's just about ready," I answer.

"Great," she says, sitting down wearily on one of the kitchen chairs and taking off her shoes. "Where's Chris?"

"Out back, playing Almighty Rat with some friend of his."

"Oh! That must be Nolan. Is he staying for dinner?"

"I don't know. I'll ask." I go out the back door and stand on the deck. "Hey, Nolan," I yell. The two of them stop karate-chopping each other and turn to look. "Would you like to stay for dinner?"

Nolan looks at Chris, then back to me. "What are you having?" he asks, sounding strangely suspicious.

"Lasagna," I answer. Picky little kid.

"Oh. No thanks," he says, and launches himself back at Chris. The two of them collapse into a snarling, giggling heap, and I go back inside.

"No, he's not staying," I tell Mom.

"OK," she says with a sigh. "I'm just going up to get changed."

When she comes back down, she's wearing jeans and a sweat shirt. The timer for the lasagna goes off.

"I'll get Chris," she says, and disappears out the back door. I look out the kitchen window. When Chris sees her, his face bursts into this huge grin and he runs over to hug her. Nolan says something and takes off through the side gate. Watching Chris and Mom together, I'm struck by how much he takes after her—they're both dark and stocky, and their eyes are the same hazel colour. I take more after my dad—I'm tall and thin, with dark brown hair and blue eyes. Aside from the hair colour, you'd never know that I'm related to Mom and Chris.

After we finish dinner, it's time to clean up. Chris clears, I wash, and Mom dries. It's a good routine—Chris has the attention span of a gerbil like most kids his age, so we don't expect him to do actual chores yet. The couple of times we'd asked him to help out with something more challenging, he'd lost interest after a few minutes and wandered off, leaving whatever it was half-done. I don't mind washing up actually; I get some kind of weird kick out of seeing the dirty dishes slide under the bubbles and come out all shiny. Who knows, right? I'm just starting on the cutlery, which I always leave for last, when Mom puts down her tea towel.

"Do you have any plans for tomorrow after school?" she asks.

"No, I thought you were working late. Why?"

"Well, I was thinking we could do a fun mother-daughter shopping and dinner thing. It's been a while. Chris is going to Nolan's right after school for a sleepover, so we could hang out," she says, smiling hopefully.

"Great," I reply. "Sounds like fun." I'm kind of surprised—Mom usually works late on Fridays, so we never get to just 'hang out'. I know some people would rather die than spend time with their parents, but I really admire my Mom—she's had to sacrifice so much since Dad died, and she's worked hard to give us a decent life. I know I can be pretty cynical and negative about a lot of things, but I respect my Mom.

"Wonderful," she says, and flicks the tea towel at me, grinning. "I'll pick you up from school, then."

"So are you OK with Chris sleeping over at Nolan's?" I ask, putting the knives and forks in the soapy water. "That kid is a bit strange, you know." That's an understatement—I predict that under Nolan's high school year book picture it will say, "Most likely to be an internet creeper".

"I know, but Chris likes him, and he needs to start developing outside interests. Nolan's mom is on Parent Council at the school. She seems nice—and responsible—and we both thought it would be a good idea to get the boys together. Maybe Chris will be a good influence on him," she laughs. "Finish up the cutlery and I'll put it away later, if you don't mind. I have a bit of paperwork to take care of before bed."

"No problem," I answer. She's right about Chris. He's really shy, always has been, so I guess it's a good thing that he's making friends, even if it is with a weird kid like Nolan. I can't help worrying though—Chris has never slept over at anyone's house before. What if he gets scared, or sick, or needs to come home? What if Nolan's parents are really axe murderers and not responsible members of Parent Council? I know I'm overprotective of him, and I worry too much, but in a lot of ways, I'm more his mother than Mom. It's not her fault that she's away so much, but for years now, I've been the one who got him up and dressed in the morning, fixed him a snack after school, made sure his homework was done—he's my responsibility as much as anyone's. Plus, like I said, I love him, even if he drives me crazy sometimes.

◆ ◆ ◆

It's Friday afternoon, last period of the day. Mr. Hummel is my science teacher. He fascinates me. He's little and pale and has blonde hair. I don't know how he does it, but he always looks exactly the same. His hair never seems to get any longer, and it never looks like it's just been cut either. He always wears dress pants, a dress shirt, and a tie, no matter how hot the weather is. On Fridays, all the other teachers dress down, and show up wearing jeans and sweatshirts. Once, I passed my art teacher in the hall on a Friday, and he was so dressed down that I swear to God I thought he was some homeless guy who had wandered into the building. Mr. Hummel's only concession to dress-down Fridays is to lose the tie. Same dress pants, same dress shirt, but no tie on Fridays. You'd think a guy who seems so uptight would be a real jerk, but he's not. He's very serious and formal all the time, but he's never mean. And every once in a while, he'll make a joke, and you know there's more to him.

When the bell rings, Mr. Hummel calls out over the general chaos of kids trying to leave as fast as possible. "Have a great weekend everyone—and don't forget about the unit test on Monday!"

I make my way to my locker through the mass of eager, weekend-hungry bodies. I'm just putting away the books I don't need when there's a husky voice in my ear. "Hey, Cass."

I turn, and Tommy Fillmore is right in my personal space. He's so creepy. I know that a lot of girls think he's hot, but there's just something about him that turns me off. I smile coldly at him.

"Hi, Tommy. What do you want?"

"You, baby," he replies, trying to sound sexy. God, how gross. Ignoring him, I turn back to my locker, and close it. He's still standing there, a little unsure of himself now. I sling my backpack over my shoulder and start to walk away.

"Hold up, Cass!" he calls, sounding angry at the obvious brush-off.

I turn around and stare at him. He's got his confidence back now, and swaggers towards me.

"So there's a party at Jared's tomorrow night. You going?" he asks. Give me a break. The last thing I need is some big, full-of-himself, hormone-driven jock mooning over me. Maybe he's just asking out of curiosity. Maybe he needs a ride. "Cuz I thought if you were, we could go together." This is sounding more like a date every minute. I say nothing. He starts to look confused, like he can't believe that I'm not jumping at the chance to go out with him. He continues on as if he thinks maybe I don't understand. "I'm asking you if—"

"I have plans," I interrupt. "Sorry." I turn and walk away down the hall, leaving him standing there, with a ticked-off look on his face. I don't feel bad—I'm sure he'll get over it quickly, and hook up with Suneeta or Missy, or any of the dozens of girls at our school who think he's all that. I go out the main door and Mom's waiting in the car.

Chapter 2

I am still in a state of shock, angry, betrayed, and confused all at the same time. How could she have done this?

Mom and I had a great time shopping. We hit all my favourite stores, and Mom never complained, even though the styles are nothing like what she would wear. She even paid for a really beautiful sweater that I'd tried on, knowing that it was more than I could afford. Everything was just perfect. After shopping, we went to an expensive Italian restaurant that serves gourmet pizza, and she told me to order whatever I wanted. I should have been suspicious at this point, noticed her nervous laughter, wondered at the money she was spending—between her salary and the money I give her, we get by, but we don't have enough extra for this kind of outing. But I was having so much fun, it never even occurred to me that there was something more going on.

We'd just finished our salads, and were waiting for the pizza to arrive. I'd ordered something called a Bellissima Primo, thin crust piled high with feta cheese, sun-dried tomatoes, sweet peppers, and all kinds of other things you never get on frozen pizza at home. My mouth was watering in anticipation.

Mom said, "Cass, I'm so glad we could spend this time together—"

"Me, too," I replied, looking around for our waitress to appear with dinner.

"—because there's something I need to talk to you about."

The sound of her voice made me focus my attention on her. She was staring down, fidgeting with her napkin, twisting the fabric and untwisting it.

"What's wrong?" I asked. She'd gone pale. What was she going to tell me? Did she have some kind of terrible illness, was that it? Was she going to die too, and leave Chris and me alone? They'd separate us and put us in foster care—I was starting to panic. "Mom, what is it?!" My voice had gotten louder. The people at the next table were looking at me.

"No, Cass, wait, it's nothing terrible," she said, making eye contact and trying to smile. "In fact, it's kind of a good thing, I think."

"What is it then?" I started to relax a little and smiled. "You had me worried for a minute."

"Well—," she hesitated, then sighed. "I've been meaning to tell you this for a while now, but the time just never seemed right. But you need to know, and I hope you'll be happy for me. I didn't like keeping it a secret from you, but I know how close you and your father were. The truth is—" She stopped again, as if summoning up all of her courage, then just blurted out in one long string, "You might have heard me mention my friend Grant from work, well, he's become more than a friend, in fact we've been seeing each other pretty regularly and things have gotten serious, so it's time that you and Chris met him, you'll like him I know, he's a wonderful man..." She trailed off, and looked at me for my reaction.

I was confused. What was she saying? "What do you mean, you've been seeing someone regularly? When do you see him?" I couldn't understand what she was talking about. She worked late most nights, and for a few months now, her Saturdays had been taken up with a course that was supposed to help her get a promotion at work, so when could she possibly have time to see anyone?

She blushed, and then giggled a little, in a bizarre, schoolgirl way. "Well, to be honest, we sometimes go out after work. And those Saturday classes? Well... they finished a while ago. I didn't want to keep this from you, but I wasn't sure you'd understand."

"Understand?" I repeated. It was starting to sink in. My mom, who I admired and trusted, had just admitted to me that she'd been sneaking around with some stranger, behind our backs. All those times when I felt so sorry for her having to work such long hours to support us, and I gave up sports and clubs and being with friends to take care of Chris—all that time, she'd been with some guy! The Saturdays when it was just Chris and me, fending for ourselves, just so she could "see someone"—and what about Dad? Had she forgotten about him?! Suddenly, I didn't want any gourmet pizza—I couldn't have swallowed it if I tried, my stomach was so knotted up.

Mom was looking at me hopefully. "Yes, I understand," I said. And I did understand. I understood that I'd been screwed over and taken advantage of by the one person I thought I could count on.

Mom sat back in her chair and visibly relaxed. "Oh, Cass, I'm so glad! This is great. So—I was thinking, you know, it's your birthday next week, what a great time for you and Chris to meet Grant. We'll go to The Golden Dragon—I know it's your favourite—and you can get to know each other. I know you'll like him. So it's all settled then!"

I felt numb. Then the waitress arrived with our dinner. "Here you go—enjoy!!" she chirped. I looked at the plate she put in front of me. What a fool I'd been, letting myself get bought off with pizza and a new sweater.

Needless to say, I didn't eat much. Everything was tasteless. When Mom questioned it, I told her I'd splurged on fries and gravy at the cafeteria at lunchtime. The waitress boxed up my pizza to take home — I felt like throwing it in the garbage, but I thought Chris might want to try it. He'd never had 'gourmet pizza' before either. I spent the car ride home worrying about how Chris was going to react to the "good news". I was glad now that he was at Nolan's — it would give me a chance to figure things out. When we pulled into the driveway, Mom hesitated before shutting off the car.

"Are you sure you're OK with this, Cass? You've been really quiet."

"Everything's fine, great," I answered. I didn't know what else she wanted from me, so I just looked at her and smiled. Then I went into the house, put the pizza in the refrigerator, went to my room, and shut the door so I could cry.

◆　◆　◆

On Saturday, I can barely concentrate at work. The mall is crazy with people and You Jane store has been doing incredible business all day, but I'm only half-here. What with Chris still at Nolan's for the day, and Mom going to her "course" (which she's stopped referring to as a course now, and just said she was going to see Grant and tell him the good news), I decided to call into work early and see if I could get a longer shift, rather than spend the day alone obsessing about things. I shouldn't have bothered because I can't stop thinking about what Mom had told me. Who is this Grant guy anyway? How could Mom just forget about Dad like that? I know it's been a few years since he died, but isn't it still some kind of betrayal? If she really loved

Dad, why not be satisfied with the years they had together? She still has us and we thought we had her. I want to be mature about this, but I just feel so used. And what does she think—we'll just accept this guy as our 'new Dad'? As if anything could take Dad's place. I'm so full of conflicting emotions that I just want to scream.

At break time, Clara comes over to talk to me. She's a lot of fun to work with; that is when I'm not in this kind of mood. She's pretty edgy—she has a lot of facial piercings, and short, spiky pink hair. I, on the other hand, have no piercings at all, except for my ears. To be honest, I like the look of a pierced eyebrow, but I'm terrified that if I had one, I'd get something caught on it and accidentally rip it out. Just the thought of it makes me feel a little sick. Today, Clara's wearing some kind of neo-bondage style dress that she definitely didn't buy at You Jane. We're only supposed to wear things that we sell here, but our boss, Jim, usually takes Saturdays off, and the manager, Chrissie, doesn't really notice. She's a complete airhead, but she's Jim's niece, so as long as nobody's stealing from the till, Jim puts her in charge on weekends.

"Did you hear about the party tonight?" Clara asks, sitting down and opening a huge lunch bag. She's always eating. I don't know where she puts it, she's so tiny. She pulls a sandwich out, her third since 10 o'clock and starts to chew.

"You mean the one at Jared's?" I reply.

She nods and mumbles through her sandwich, "That's the one. You going? I can give you a ride if you need it."

I'm about to say no, but then I stop. Why shouldn't I go to a party? It's about time I had a little fun too.

"Yeah, I was thinking about going. A ride would be great, if you don't mind," I say.

"Excellent! I didn't want to go by myself. It's always so weird just showing up at a party solo, if you know what I mean."

I give her my address, and she says she'll come by at 7:30. I wonder what Mom will say, but I don't really care.

After work, the bus from the mall is noisy and packed, and when I walk into the house, it's like an oasis of calm. Then I hear voices coming from the kitchen and I stiffen. She hasn't brought him home, has she?! But when I go into the kitchen, it's only Mom and Chris. Chris is sitting on a stool at the island, wearing his Almighty Rat suit and talking and gesturing with his hands in an excited way. Mom's listening intently, as she stirs a pot of pasta on the stove. Chris spins on the stool when he hears me come in.

"Cass!" He jumps off the stool, runs over and gives me a big hug. I hug him back and kiss him on the top of his head. Mom looks over at us and smiles.

"Did you have a good time at Nolan's?" I ask.

"Yeah, it was awesome! He has a PlayStation with some really cool games, and we had pork chops for dinner, and we stayed up late, and I got to sleep in a sleeping bag on the floor!"

"Wow!" I exclaim. "Sounds like a great time. Are you tired?"

"Nope!" he answers, and starts jumping around the kitchen doing Rat-style karate chops.

"Take it easy, honey," Mom laughs. "Dinner's almost ready — go wash up." Chris runs out of the kitchen, yelling 'Hyah!' and chopping the air. Mom turns to me.

"Did you have a good day at work?" she asks.

"Yeah, it was fine," I answer, then quickly add, "Clara from work asked me if I wanted to go to a party with her tonight. She said she'd pick me up at 7:30. I hope that's OK."

Mom looks doubtful. "I don't know, Cass. Whose party is it? Where is it? Will it be supervised?"

She has a lot of nerve questioning me like this, as though I'm up to no good. Especially the way she's been lying about her whereabouts lately. But I just smile and tell her the details, making up the part about how Jared's parents will be there. I have no idea whether they will or not, but I'm determined to go to this party. I don't want to spend another Saturday night watching TV with Mom and Chris. Finally, she says, "Well, all right. Just keep your cell phone turned on."

We sit down to dinner, the three of us, and as she's dishing out the spaghetti, she says, quite casually, "So, I told Chris about Grant."

"Oh?" I answer. I look at Chris, but he isn't paying attention—he's too busy slurping individual strands of spaghetti into his mouth, and getting sauce all over his chin.

"You two really are the best kids. He seems fine with it too." She smiles and passes a basket of rolls. I love how she assumes I'm fine with this.

"Fine with what?" Chris says through a huge mouthful of pasta.

"Chris, slow down, you'll choke. Fine about Grant," Mom says cheerfully.

"Oh yeah!" Chris turns to me, swallowing his food. "Mom has a boyfriend! We get to meet him at your birthday party."

Boyfriend! I can't believe how this is all being normalized so fast. I know Chris doesn't really remember Dad, and I know he thinks all news is good news until you tell him differently, but I'm shocked at how excited he seems about it. I shove down my spaghetti and roll, then excuse myself to get ready for the party.

I have no idea what to wear. What do people wear to parties? I don't want to be either over- or under-dressed, so I go with skinny jeans and my new sweater. I've never wanted to stand out—God knows I hate being the centre of attention. That's why this whole archaeology thing has been so awful. As soon as people hear that, they assume you're some kind of genius, and start envisioning you as an Indiana Jones type character—or in my case, Lara Croft, Tomb Raider, since I'm a girl. Why did I say archaeology?

Why not lawyer? Still respectable, but run of the mill enough that no one cares. To be honest, I find the idea of participating in a dig somewhere in an exotic foreign country a little fascinating, but that's just dreaming. Better to be realistic and admit that it's never going to happen. At any rate, I have a party to go to, and I'm going to have fun. At least that's what I tell myself.

Clara rolls up to the door a little after 7:30 pm. She's a couple of years older than I am, and has her own car, an ancient, beat-up Chevy that I can't believe will actually get us to Jared's. I'm relieved to see that she's wearing jeans too, although hers have bondage-type lacing, and leather trim. Mom's fussing in a disturbingly maternal way—I pretend not to notice, and promise to text her when we get there.

When we get in the car, Clara says, "God, your mother's a little uptight—she was acting like you'd never gone to a party before."

"Actually," I answer, a little embarrassed, "I don't get out much." I almost tell her the whole sordid tale, of me sacrificing my social life to take care of my brother while Mom was at "work", but I don't know Clara very well, and I'm not that talkative at the best of times.

"Well, you're out now, and it's going to be epic!" she shouts. Maybe she doesn't get out much either—she seems way too excited about this.

Chapter 3

It is hard to miss the house where the party is. Loud, pounding music, bright lights, people milling around on the lawn — yep, this must be Jared's place, and I have grave doubts that his parents are here, supervising the destruction of their rose bushes. I text Mom and let her know that everything is good, that Jared's parents have ordered pizza for everyone. I hate lying, but right now, I don't feel particularly like I owe her total honesty. Clara grabs my arm as we walk up the sidewalk, and says, "This is great — what a way to end a crappy week!"

I feel like I have to ask. "Why was your week crappy?"

She sighs and stops. "My mother," she says. "I know it's hard for you to understand, since your own mom seems to care so much about you, but my mother and I do not get along. We never have. And ever since my Dad took off, it's been one guy after the other. I caught the latest jerk staring down my top, and when I told her, she freaked out and called me a liar. It didn't surprise me, but then she told me I have two weeks to get my own place. I'm worried about my little sister. What'll happen to her if I leave, and 'Mr. Wonderful' starts up with her? She's only 10. You're so lucky, Cass, you really don't know."

No, she really doesn't know. At least she's always known she couldn't rely on her mom. How would she like to spend almost 17 years believing that she could, and then suddenly find out it was all a lie? I'm not sure how to respond, so I just say, "Wow, that really sucks."

We start walking up the sidewalk again. "Yeah, it really does," she replies. "So what's your Dad like? I bet he's nice. Too bad he wasn't there when we left."

This is always the awkward moment. I say it as simply as I can. "He died a few years ago."

"Oh man, I'm sorry, Cass—I didn't know," she says, as we dodge some kid running across the lawn. "God, I wish my dad was dead," she continues. "You know that asshole completely forgot my birthday again this year... oh crap, I'm such an idiot. That was really insensitive, right?"

"Don't worry about it," I say and smile at her.

After being here for over an hour, I was ready to leave about an hour ago. People are yelling, smoking, drinking, the music is too loud, and I don't know anyone. We were no sooner in the door when Clara spotted someone she knew. She said, "I'll be right back," and that was the last I've seen of her. The smoke is starting to get really thick at this point, and I don't think it's all cigarette smoke, either. I don't know what Mom will say if I come home smelling like the inside of a hippy's van, so I make my way out back. I go through the kitchen, looking for a door. I recognize some of the people from school, but there are a lot of unfamiliar faces, too. Just then, somebody grabs my elbow. Clara's back, looking a little glassy-eyed and holding something that looks like a cigarette, but which I know isn't. She pulls me out the door and onto the patio.

"There you are," she says sleepily. "I've been looking for you everywhere. I brought you something. We can share it." She waggles the joint in my face, then lights it up and inhales deeply. Then she holds it out to me. "Come on, Cass, a little bit won't hurt." I've never tried any kind of drug before, except for the prescription kind, and the only alcohol I've ever had is a half glass of wine with Christmas dinner. I don't even like the taste. "Really," she repeats, "it's good stuff. Don't make me smoke it all by myself."

I've never been one to bow to peer pressure. In fact, most of the time, I couldn't care less what other people think. But suddenly, I want to try it. Hell, why not? If Mom could have this whole secret life, then why couldn't I do something exciting too? I take the joint from her and hold it up to my lips. I have no idea how to do this—I've never tried cigarettes either. I put it tentatively to my lips and inhale. Immediately, I know it's a mistake. I start coughing and hacking, and my eyes are tearing like crazy. "Oh—cough—my—hack—God—cough!" I sputter out. "Here, take it!" I shove it back at her, while trying to wipe my eyes clear.

She laughs. "Suit yourself! See ya later!" And with that, she disappears back into the house, leaving me alone. I make my way over to a picnic table in an alcove off the patio and sit down, still coughing and clearing my throat. Then it suddenly occurs to me, in a panic of realization. Clara is my ride! How am I going to get home? She's stoned, and obviously can't drive, so not only do I have to worry about me, but now I have to worry about getting her home safely too. The night is getting worse by the second.

I lean back to consider my options and look up into the night sky. It's so clear—the stars are all out, and it's really peaceful back here. I start thinking about star-gazing with Dad. For my ninth birthday, he got me a telescope, not one of those kiddy ones but a real telescope with a 3 inch reflector lens. Whenever Mom was busy at night with Chris, who had a lot of health problems when he was a baby because he was born so early, Dad and I would get out the telescope and set it up on the back deck, and just look at the stars for hours. He taught me the names of all the constellations we could see, and we kept a stargazing journal to keep track. I don't know where it is now. After he died, we sold the telescope at a yard sale. I don't like to look at stars anymore.

By this point, my head is starting to swim so I put my knees up and rest it on them. After a few minutes, I'm beginning to feel a little better and decide to go back inside. When I look up, the entrance to the alcove is blocked by a back-lit figure. I squint and a voice speaks;

"Hey there, gorgeous. I've been looking for you. I thought you said you had other plans." Tommy Fillmore. Great—the last thing I need.

I clear my throat and wipe my eyes. "Plans change. So here I am. What do you want?"

He comes closer. He reeks of alcohol. "Same thing as always, of course. You."

I stand up. "Well, you know, that's never going to happen." I want to go past him, but as I try to squeeze through the narrow gap between him and the alcove entrance, he grabs my arm.

"C'mon, Cass—you know how hot I think you are."

His face is right up near mine, and his breath is making me queasy. He pulls me up against him.

"Tommy, let go—you're hurting my arm!" I try to yank it away, but he's really strong and determined. He pulls me back to him, and when he speaks, he sounds furious. "You know, you think you're so special, the way you act like I'm dirt under your feet. Well, we'll see who's dirt now." He grabs the back of my head with his other hand, and starts to pull my face towards his. I can't make him let go, so I do the only thing I can think of. I kick him as hard as I can in the shin. He yells in pain, and immediately lets go of me. I stand there, breathing hard, eyes darting wildly, trying to find a way around him and out of the alcove. Then before I can do anything, he yells "You bitch!" and backhands me in the face. I taste blood and my eyes go out of focus. I stagger backwards into the far corner of the alcove, reeling from the blow. No one has ever hit me before. I realize that I'm terrified. Just as I'm about to scream for help, Tommy suddenly goes flying into the picnic table headfirst.

"Hey there, Fillmore. Trying to prove you're a man again?" I try to place the voice, and as the figure comes into focus, I'm shocked. It's Danny Stryker. The green mohawk is a dead giveaway. Tommy picks himself up and turns around, ready to fight back, but when he realizes who it is, he stops. I'm confused—Tommy actually looks a little afraid. Danny says, "Get your ass out of here, Fillmore." And with that, Tommy staggers out of the alcove without a word. He doesn't look back, but just keeps walking.

I realize that the inside of my mouth is cut up from Tommy's slap. I can't even imagine what I'm going to say when I get home. My eyes well up with tears. Danny comes over and leads me to the picnic table bench, where we both sit down.

"Are you okay?" he asks. He looks concerned, really worried. Can this be the same Danny Stryker from my English class, the one who keeps to himself and never talks to anyone?

I nod my head. "Nothing permanent," I say, and try to smile, but I'm not up to it. "I just need to sit here for a minute." He nods and leans back against the picnic table. I stare straight ahead. Neither of us says anything for a while. Finally, he speaks.

"Beautiful night," he says. "I mean the stars and all that."

I nod in agreement, then it all overwhelms me, and I start to really cry. I'm not crying so much about what happened with Tommy, as much as just everything. After a while, I open my purse and hunt for a tissue. "God, I'm a mess," I say. He misunderstands.

"No, you look fine, really. You're not swelling up that much at all. If you ice it, it won't even be noticeable in the morning."

"No," I half-laugh, "I mean, I'M a mess, everything is a mess." I wipe my nose in a very un-ladylike way, but at this point it doesn't seem to make a lot of difference.

"Tommy's a jerk. Always has been," Danny says, looking at me searchingly. I look back, and realize that I've never really looked at him before. I mean, I see him in my English class and in the halls, but I've never actually looked closely at him. He's good-looking, and even though he's not super-tall, he's really athletic. I'm still having trouble making sense of what just happened, so I finally just come out with it.

"Why did Tommy take off when you showed up? He seemed almost scared when he realized it was you. I really thought he would have killed you for pushing him into the picnic table."

Danny laughs. "Oh, Tommy and I go back a long way. All the way back to kung fu class when we were kids. He stopped taking lessons after tenth grade and I didn't. I've kicked his ass a few times in the sparring ring, and he knows that I'm a black belt now."

"Seriously?!" I say, completely surprised. "I didn't know that."

"Well, I don't make a big deal out of it. I switched to kickboxing last year, and I've been competing a lot. That's why I miss so much school. I don't want to brag, but I'm actually second in my weight class nationally." He smiles shyly, and stares straight ahead.

"That's really impressive," I reply. I mean it. I am really impressed, especially since his quiet reputation just saved me from God knows what might have happened with Tommy.

"Yeah, well, anyway... So, you said everything is a mess. Why?"

I barely know him, but somehow I feel like we've been friends forever. Still, I don't want to get into all the gory details right now, so I deal with the immediate problem.

"My ride is stoned. So not only do I have no way home, I have to figure out how to get her keys away from her."

"No problem," Danny says. "I know Clara pretty well. I'll get her keys, then I can drive both of you home. I only live 5 houses down from her." So for the second time in one night, this total stranger has become my knight in shining armour. It isn't until later that it occurs to me that I didn't tell him Clara was my ride.

I got home after midnight and managed to get by Mom quickly. She was asleep on the couch with the TV on when I came in and barely lifted her head to ask, "Have a good time?" before dozing off again.

I called out, "Yeah, good night" on my way upstairs, trying to sound normal, then shut myself in my room and waited for her to go to bed. Finally, around 1:30 am, she made her way upstairs. I've been sitting here ever since, trying to make sense of everything that happened at the party. I get my pyjamas on and try to put my clothes away, but my hands are still shaky. I sit down at my dressing table—a really beautiful, antique vanity with a big mirror that Mom and Dad bought me when I was younger. It matches the 'princess' style of the room, but I'm getting too old for that—it was so cool when I was eight, but now it just seems babyish. I look into the mirror, and I'm suddenly filled with disgust—disgust with Tommy, disgust with Clara, and most of all, disgust with myself. What was I thinking, putting myself in that kind of situation? And what would have happened if Danny hadn't come along when he did? I scrutinize my face for signs of bruising, and feel the cut inside my mouth with my tongue. In the reflection, I can see the pile of clothes behind me, the new sweater on top, the sweater that Tommy Fillmore was touching. I can't stand it anymore. How can I ever wear it again? It seems tainted, soiled by his hands and my mom's betrayal. I grab the sweater off the floor, and before I realize what I'm doing, I'm out the back door and into the back yard. I grab a shovel and start to dig.

Chapter 4

onday morning I brace myself as I walk into school. I'm sure that the rumour mill is already at work, and I'll be subject to all kinds of nasty, exaggerated stories about me and Tommy, likely generated by Tommy himself, leaving out the parts where I kicked him, and Danny scared the crap out of him, of course. But by lunchtime, I haven't heard a thing, no one has looked at me and whispered something to a friend, there are no notes being passed across any of my classrooms, no mad texting while people stare at me and snicker. I'm relieved.

Before lunch, I have English class. As usual, Danny isn't there. I feel strangely disappointed but maybe it's for the best—I really don't know how I should act when I see him anyway. We're starting *Romeo and Juliet* by William Shakespeare. As Mrs. Gilman is telling us about it, in a breathless, excited way, a lot of the kids in the class are rolling their eyes and groaning. Personally, I like Shakespeare. The way the language flows is really gorgeous sometimes, although it can be hard to understand. Last summer, I tried reading *Hamlet*, a play about a guy whose dad dies, and his uncle marries his mother. Right now, I can completely relate to how he felt. There was this one great line where Hamlet says about his dad, "He was a man, take him for all in all, I shall not look upon his like again." In other words, his dad was just a man, but he was special. I repeat that line in my head sometimes, when I think about my own dad. Half-way through Mrs. Gilman's "Shakespeare is sooo wonderful" speech, Danny walks into class, and sits down at his desk by the door. Without missing a beat, Mrs. Gilman walks over to his desk and holds out her hand. He gives her his late slip and she turns away, still talking. While her back is turned, he suddenly looks over in my direction. We make eye contact, and he mouths, "Hey." I feel myself starting to turn red, but I manage to mouth "Hey" back and give him a little half-wave, which immediately attracts the attention of everyone around me. I can sense the eyebrows being raised, and the looks being passed back and forth. Danny, meanwhile, smiles, then turns back to face front just as Mrs. Gilman whips around. He stretches out his legs and leans back casually, and she gives him a hard look before continuing on. Right before the bell is about to ring, Mrs. Gilman gets a call.

"Cass," she says, "Mr. Pratt wants to see you in the guidance office. You can go now, since class is almost over." God, there's nothing I hate worse than having to get up and walk in front of a room full of people who have nothing better to do than watch you go by. Especially today.

As I pass Danny, he straightens up in his desk and whispers, "Cass!" I stop and he says quietly, "Meet me at lunch?" Aware of all the eyes on me, I nod quickly and go out the door.

Mr. Pratt's plants look as healthy as ever. I have no idea what he wants, but as I walk into his office, he looks very pleased with himself.

"Hello, Cass!" he says expansively, and motions to a chair. "Sit, please!" He seems barely able to contain himself.

I dump my knapsack on the floor and plunk myself down. He keeps looking at me with a big smile on his face.

"So, Mr. Pratt," I say, "you wanted to see me?" I have to admit that my curiosity is piqued. At first I was worried that somehow he had heard about what happened at the party, but how could he have? And if he had, he wouldn't be this happy about it, would he?

Pratt reaches for something on his cluttered desk. "Guess what I have here?" He waves some paper in front of me.

"Gosh, I really don't know, Mr. Pratt," I say in a fake, I-can-hardly-wait kind of way. "What is it?"

"Well," he begins, in a hushed voice, as though it's a big secret, "I have something very exciting for you. I don't know if I ever told you this, but I have a very good friend who works at the university in the archaeology department..." I do know this—he mentions it like every other sentence when we're talking about my 'future'. "...and every year, his department runs an archaeology camp up north for children ages 8 – 13. They normally only hire graduating high school students, but I've told him so much about you that he's willing to make an exception! Isn't that wonderful?"

I'm confused. "Hire for what?" I ask. "Exception for what?"

"Well, to help run the camp, of course! Like a—a—camp counsellor, you know, helping the kids with the dig, and so on. It's for the month of July—the kids come for two weeks at a time, and they dig for artefacts at an early Pioneer site. What do you think? I have the application right here. All you have to do is fill it out—the job is as good as yours."

"So," I try to wrap my brain around what he's saying, "you have an application for me to work as a counsellor at an archaeology summer camp up north?"

"Yes!" he replies. "The pay's not much, but think of the experience. When you apply to university next year, it will certainly give you an advantage over the other applicants!" He pauses and his face suddenly falls. "I thought you'd be excited, Cass—is something wrong?"

If he only knew. How on earth does he think I can just take off for an entire month? Who would look after Chris? Besides, the archaeology thing isn't something I was ever serious about... although the idea of working at a dig up north with kids Chris's age does sound kind of fun.

"No, it's great, Mr. Pratt. I just have to think about it—there's a lot to consider. I really appreciate you looking into this for me." And I do, appreciate it I mean. I suddenly feel really crappy that I can't just say 'Fantastic', grab the application, and fill it in right then and there.

"OK, I understand," he says, handing me the paperwork. "The deadline is the end of the month, but if you decide you want to do this, make sure you submit it well before then—there's a lot of competition for the positions."

"All right," I say, taking the application from him. "Thanks, Mr. Pratt." I go out into the hall and lean against the wall, looking at what he's given me. In addition to the application, there's a brochure about the camp with pictures of kids digging, campers and counsellors sitting around a fire toasting marshmallows, and samples of some of the artefacts that had been found at the sites. It actually looks cool. I start imagining myself with a group of little Chrises and Nolans, supervising a dig and singing camp songs. Then I stop myself. What's the point? It's never going to happen. With Mom working through the summer, she'll never let me go—she needs me to look after Chris. I sigh and head towards the cafeteria to find Danny.

I have no idea where Danny eats lunch since I don't know who he hangs around with, so I go on a tour of the school. He's not in the lower hall with the hipsters, not hanging out by the gym with the jocks, and not up on the third floor with the gamers. I find Danny in the cafeteria (who knew?!), eating a protein bar and discussing the finer points of vitamin supplements with a scary-looking guy who has a brush cut and a tattoo on his neck. When Danny notices that I've sat down next to him, he looks at me and smiles.

"Hey Cass," he says, and indicates the other guy, "this is my friend, Miles." Miles? I was expecting something more like 'Brutus' or 'Killer'. Miles has muscles on top of muscles and looks mean. But then he smiles at me, and I notice that the tattoo on his neck says 'Faith' in beautiful, scrolled lettering.

"Hi," he says in a quiet voice.

"Hi Miles," I reply. I notice that there's a pamphlet on the table between them advertising an upcoming kick-boxing tournament. "So, are you into martial arts too?"

"Nah," he laughs shyly, "none of that sissy stuff for me." He reaches across the table and gives Danny a friendly punch in the arm. "I'm a wrestler."

"Sissy?!" Danny laughs. "Nice try!" He punches Miles back. Miles winces and rubs his arm, still grinning.

"I know," he says. "You could kick my butt any day of the week. But one day I'll get you in the wrestling ring and then we'll see! Anyway, gotta go. Thanks for letting me know about your tournament, man. I'll be there to cheer you on. See you later." He grabs his lunch tray and leaves me alone with Danny. Suddenly I feel a little uncomfortable, kind of nervous, but I'm not sure why.

Danny leans in and says. "How are you feeling? Your face looks fine—I mean, uh, there's no bruise or anything." He stammers a bit and I realize that he seems a little nervous, too. I notice how green his eyes are, something I couldn't see the other night in the dimly lit alcove.

"No, I'm OK," I answer, then it all comes pouring out. "Listen, thanks for the other night, really, I mean, I don't know what I would have done—or what would have happened—I—anyway, thanks." I take a breath and look down at my hands. I can feel my face getting red again. I'm just not used to having people do things for me; ever since

Dad died, I've had to be the responsible one, the independent one. It feels strange having to rely on other people, embarrassing to be 'needy'.

He seems to understand, and says, "No worries. I'm just glad you and Clara got home safe. But listen, that's what I need to talk to you about—Clara."

Glad for the distraction, I answer, "Sure, what about her? I'm still angry at her for getting wasted on Saturday. What did she think, she was just going to drive us both home like that?!"

"I know," Danny says. "It was really stupid of her, but something happened on Sunday, and I'm worried."

"What happened?" Danny doesn't look like much of a worrier, so the concern in his voice has my attention.

"Well, it was early Sunday morning, like 5:00 am or something. I heard all this commotion down the street, sirens and yelling, so I got up and went outside. There were cops outside of Clara's house. They had her mom's boyfriend in handcuffs, her mom was on the porch screaming, and Clara and her little sister Lindsay were standing with some official-looking woman. Then the cops shoved the boyfriend into a squad car, and Clara and Lindsay got into the woman's car. Clara's mom was still screaming, something about getting a lawyer, and Clara never setting foot in the house again. Then the cops and the other car drove off, and she went in the house and slammed the door. A little while later, she got into Clara's car and took off." Danny rubs his forehead and looks at me expectantly. This sounds worse than serious, and I remember what Clara told me about her mom's boyfriend trying to look down her top.

"Clara told me that guy was a total creep." I repeat to Danny what she told me on Saturday. "I know she was really worried about her little sister being in the same house as him. God, what could have happened?!"

"I don't know," Danny answers, "but there's been no sign of Clara or Lindsay since then."

"Well, we're both scheduled to work tomorrow night. Maybe I can find out then, make sure she's OK." I hesitate. "If you wanted to, you could come by on my break. I usually take it around 7:30."

"Yeah, that'd be good." He smiles at me, then lightly touches my face and looks serious. "Has Tommy said anything to you today?"

"No," I reply, "I haven't even seen him yet." I'm actually dreading an encounter with him, but I don't let Danny know that.

"Well," he says. "If he bothers you at all, let me know right away. Promise?"

I feel strange—I've never felt the need for a protector. I've always been able to handle things on my own, and I'm just about to tell Danny that when I remember the feeling of Tommy's hand gripping my arm. Suddenly, I'm glad to have Danny looking out for me. "I promise," I say.

"Good. Your little brother would be no match for Tommy," he smiles. "Gotta go to math class. See you later." I watch him go out of the cafeteria. Then it hits me—I never told him I had a little brother. How does he know so much about me? I could be completely weirded out, but something tells me that there's nothing about Danny to be afraid of.

The rest of the day passes without incident—I keep my head down, and by the time the bells rings at the end of the day, I'm ready to go home. I'm at my locker, packing up, when I see Tommy coming down the hall. My stomach does a flip, and I fumble with my knapsack. He has his eyes straight ahead, seemingly not seeing me. But as he passes by, eyes still looking down the hall, he mutters "Bitch" through gritted teeth. Not loud enough for anyone else to hear, just me. Well, if that's the best he's got, I can deal with it. No need to tell Danny and cause any more conflict. I lock up my locker and walk out in the other direction.

Chapter 5

Mom comes home late—having a good time with Grant, I imagine, while Chris and I work on his math homework. I make a simple dinner of chicken and potatoes, which Mom raves over. I swear she's trying to stay on my good side—why ruin a good thing, right? I used to look forward to coming home and having a "family" dinner, but now it just seems so fake. And I keep imagining the day that Grant is sitting in Dad's place, asking inane questions like 'How was school?' and laughing with Chris and Mom like he's the man of the house. Talk about spoiling your appetite. Of course, I'm polite and smile through everything the way I always do, but I can barely gag the food down.

As Mom serves dessert (pre-packaged butter tarts), I decide to broach the subject of the archaeology camp. I know it's a long shot, but I've been thinking about it ever since I got home, and despite myself, I've been getting a little excited at the idea of actually doing it, of finding a focus. Why not archaeology, anyway? I know I've been using it for ages to get people off my back, but really—why not?

I can totally see myself in some foreign land, digging up long-lost treasures — OK, let's not get carried away, it's only a camp up north, I tell myself, but still...

"So, Mom, I was talking to Mr. Pratt today," I venture.

"Your guidance counsellor? What about?" She takes a bite of her tart and hands Chris a napkin. As usual, he's holding his tart too tightly and it's oozing all over his hands. I think he does it on purpose because, like most boys his age, he loves ooze.

"Well, he has this friend who's a professor at the university. He runs an archaeology camp up north in the summer, and he could give me a job as a camp counsellor for the month of July. It sounds like a great opportunity."

Mom puts down the butter tart and sighs. "Oh, Cass, I don't know. What about Chris?"

We both look at Chris. He's busy licking the tart filling off his hands and is wearing the napkin on his head like a hat. I can't help but snicker, and Mom smiles and says, "Chris, come on!"

He looks up, all innocent. "What?"

"Anyway, honey," Mom continues, "I just don't see how it would work. Maybe you could do it next year, when Chris is older, and then we can think about finding someone else to watch him for a few hours while I'm at work. OK?"

Exactly the answer I expected. "I guess." Even though I could have predicted what she would say, I'm still disappointed. More disappointed than I thought I would be, actually.

After dinner, I go to my room to do my own homework. I'm sitting cross-legged on my bed, struggling through verb cases 'en francais', when there's a knock and my door opens. Mom has a laundry basket tucked under her arm.

"Sorry to bother you while you're hard at work, Cass," she jokes. "I've just come to get your laundry. I thought I'd toss some of yours in with this load."

"Great, thanks," I reply. Normally, I do my own laundry, but I won't say no to someone else picking up my slack for a change. Mom heads to the closet where I keep my laundry hamper and starts pulling clothes out.

"How's the homework going?" she asks with her head still in the closet. "Having any problems?"

"No, it's fine," I answer. "Just a little French." Cute. She hasn't helped me with my homework for years. I go back to trying to demystify subjunctive, imperative, and indicative verbs. Everything is quiet.

"Cass?" She's rummaging around in the closet, looking through the clothes on the hangers. "Where's the sweater that I bought you on Friday, the one you wore to the party?" She turns around and looks at me with a perturbed expression. "It probably needs to be washed, but it's not in here. Where is it?"

Oh God. My stomach clenches and I swallow hard. What I did with that sweater was really stupid and impulsive, but it never occurred to me that she would find out. "Oh, um, it's not there?" I answer, not very convincingly.

"No, Cass, it's not," she says, looking directly at me.

"Right," I say, trying to sound light-hearted and casual. "Well, the sleeve got snagged on something at the party, and pulled some of the stitching out, so—I threw it away." If there was a prize for worst answer ever, I'd be getting it right now. I wish to God I could tell her what really happened, but that would just make a bad situation even more terrible. Mom's eyes narrow, and she says very slowly and deliberately, "Threw it away?"

"Yeah—sorry, I didn't know what else to do with it." We stare at each other. I can see the anger building up in her face. Suddenly, she throws down the laundry basket. Clothes scatter everywhere. I've never seen her this angry. With her voice bordering on outright fury, she says, "Dammit, Cass! Why on earth would you do something like that?! A snag? I could have fixed it for you! How could you just throw it away? That sweater cost a lot of money, you know that, and it's not like we're so rich that we can just go throwing things away when it suits us! I don't believe you could be so thoughtless!"

Now, I'm the one who's getting furious. She has a lot of nerve tossing our financial situation in my face. Me, who hands over most of my puny paycheque from my stupid job to support the family. Me, who's giving up the chance to get a real summer job doing something meaningful so she doesn't have to actually pay for a babysitter. All the anger I've been feeling since her revelation at dinner the other night boils over and before I realize what I'm doing, I say, very coldly, "Well, maybe we'd have more money if you were actually working overtime and going to classes to get promotions instead of screwing around with your new boyfriend." My words hang in the air between us; suddenly, I'd give anything to pull them back into my mouth but it's too late. She gasps like she's just been punched by a stranger and takes a step backwards. I drop my eyes and feel my cheeks turning red.

"Mom, I..." I don't know what to say to fix this. I look back up, and she's bending over picking up the laundry and putting it all back in the basket. "I'm sorry, I didn't mean it..."

She doesn't say anything, just keeps picking up laundry. When she straightens up, her eyes are full of tears. One escapes and slides down her face. She looks wounded and fragile.

"No, Cass, let's just leave it for now—. " Her voice breaks and she hurries out of the room. I pound the bed with my hands and then bury my face in the comforter, trying not to cry myself.

◆ ◆ ◆

Today has been pretty uneventful. Mom left early for work, probably to avoid me. I don't blame her. I looked out of the window as she was getting into the car. Her eyes were red-rimmed, and she looked like she hadn't slept much. Neither had I. As a result, I've been feeling a little wobbly and out of it all day. I wanted to talk to Danny but he wasn't in English class and I didn't see him in the cafeteria. Hopefully, he'll show up tonight at work like he said he would.

After school, I get on the city bus to the mall. The bus is packed, and I get one of the last seats, next to an old woman who's mumbling to herself. I'm pretending to be interested in the ads above the windows when someone taps me on the shoulder. I turn around — Tara Connelly and Megan Pearson from English class are sitting behind me.

"Hey Cass!" they both say at the same time.

"Hey," I say back. What do these two airheads want?

"So, Cass." says Megan. "What is the deal with you and Danny Stryker? We have to know!" They both giggle and look at each other.

"What are you talking about?" I answer. I might have known that the gossip mill would be churning, thanks to Tara and Megan.

"Come on!" exclaims Tara. "The whispering in class? Meeting in the cafeteria? Tell us all the details!"

"There aren't any 'details'," I answer. "Danny and I are friends, that's all." God, going to high school is like living in a fish bowl — everyone sees everything you do, and you can't escape.

"Just friends, huh?" Megan smirks. "Well, he is kind of hot."

"In his own freakish way," Tara says under her breath to Megan, as if I can't hear her.

"He's not a freak," I answer with a forced smile. "He's actually really nice." Why am I defending him to

Megan and Tara? They're the freaks — who cares what they think? Are we at the mall yet?

"Well, keep us posted!" they both giggle.

"Sure thing!" I reply with fake enthusiasm, and turn back around, pretending to look for something in my purse. The old woman next to me has now started singing what sounds like the theme from The Sound of Music. I look at her and she says, "Lemon!"

"Right, lemon," I answer. She's actually a better conversationalist than either Megan or Tara. Thankfully the bus pulls into the mall before she starts up with the show tunes again, and I make my way to You Jane.

When I get there, there's no sign of Clara. After my dinner break, I'm helping a woman find something "stylish" for her daughter's birthday, when I realize that Clara is over by the belts and accessories. I take the woman and her purchases to the register, and when she's gone, Clara comes over. She looks terrible, like she hasn't washed for a couple of days, and her clothes are all wrinkled.

"Hi," she says.

"Hi, Clara," I answer, pretending not to be completely dying to find out what's going on.

"Listen, I'm really sorry about the other night. What a crappy friend, huh? Sometimes things just get so awful that I do something stupid to take my mind off it. I didn't mean to drag you out, then ditch you like that."

"Seriously, it's not a problem." I mean it by this point. I'm over being angry at her and now I'm just worried about her. She has dark circles under her eyes, and her nails are chewed right down. I have to find a way to get her talking. Blunt is best, so here goes. "But I have to ask — no offence, but you look awful. Is everything OK?" I know it's not, but I have the feeling that things are worse than Danny and I thought.

Her eyes start to well up. "No," she whispers, and looks down.

"Clara, tell me what's going on. You can trust me, you know that."

"Come back to the change rooms where we can talk in private," she whispers. We both look around. Chrissie's busy with the only customer in the store, so we head to the back. When we get to the change rooms, she just kind of crumples and crouches against the wall with her face in her hands. When she finally looks up, her face is pale and her eyes look even more bloodshot. She heaves a great sigh, and I say, "Clara, God, you're freaking me out—what's going on?!"

"OK," she says finally. "You know what I told you before about my mom and her boyfriend?"

"You mean the creepy one who was staring down your top?"

"It gets worse." She sniffs and wipes the tears off her face with the back of her hand. "After the party on Saturday night, I was pretty out of it when I got home. You know that—again, I'm so sorry—"

"Clara, for the last time, stop worrying about it. What happened?"

"Well, I went to bed, and at some point, I don't know, about 4 o'clock in the morning, I woke up. I guess I heard a noise or something. Anyway, I opened my eyes, and that loser Frank was standing in my bedroom, looking down at me. I said, "What are you doing in here?!" And he said, "No one has to know, baby," with this awful look on his face. I started yelling for him to get out, and my mom came running, and Lindsay woke up, and the next thing you know, Lindsay called 911, and my mom was screaming at me, and Frank was yelling that he didn't do anything..." She stopped to take a breath. This was worse than I could ever have imagined. Suddenly my problems seemed pretty miniscule.

"Go on," I prompted her. "What happened then?"

"So the police arrive, and it's just chaos, with Mom and me screaming at each other and Lindsay crying, and Frank yelling. They take one look at Frank, and put the cuffs on. Then a social worker shows up, helps us pack what we can, and puts Lindsay and me in a car. As we're driving away, the last thing I hear Mom yelling is "You're a lying little bitch, Clara. Don't ever come back here."

"Oh my God — where did they take you?" I'm having trouble getting my mind around this — it seems like something that would happen in a movie.

"First to an office. The woman made some phone calls, and then…." She starts crying in earnest. "She said she had no choice. That Frank had a record, and Lindsay wasn't safe. They took her to a foster home, but I'm over 18, so I'm on my own."

"What did you do? Where have you been living?" I ask.

"The social worker took me to a shelter, and I stayed there on Sunday night, but it was really awful, Cass. I caught some girl going through my things, and the people there were just so — anyway, I left. I went by the house to get my car, but it was gone, and so was my mom. I was afraid she might come back though, so I slept in the park last night. What am I going to do? I have to get Lindsay back, but how can I afford an apartment? I have some money I've been saving for college, but it's not enough. I can't let her go back to Mom — she's drunk most of the time and all she cares about is her stupid boyfriend. I can take care of Lindsay myself, but I need money. Even working here full-time, I don't know if I can swing it." Her hands are shaking as she tries to wipe her eyes.

"Look," I say. "I know we don't know each other really well, but you're coming home with me. You can stay at my house until you get things figured out." I have no idea what Mom is going to say about this, but I can't stand seeing Clara so devastated.

"No, Cass, I can't do that. I'll stay in the park—the weather's not too bad. I—," She's trying to sound brave and capable, but her voice breaks and gives her away.

"No arguments," I say firmly. "It'll be fine, I promise." I have no idea if it really will be fine, but she's coming home with me.

Chapter 6

At 7:30 pm I go out into the mall for my break. I leave Clara, who's cleaned herself up and is dealing with a guy who wants acid-washed jeans—yes, acid wash—and head for the food court. I grab a soda from Mexicana Deluxe, and spot Danny at one of the few clean tables. I go over and sit down across from him.

"Hey," he smiles.

Tara might be an airhead, but she's right about one thing—Danny is kind of hot. He has this quiet confidence, and I could just about lose myself in those green eyes... Focus, Cass! I tell myself.

"Hey," I answer, trying to sound casual. I take a sip of my drink, then fill him in on what I've learned from Clara. "So, you were right—it's really serious. I told her she's coming back to stay at my house. She didn't want to at first, but I convinced her it was better than sleeping in the park."

"Yeah, those shelters are nasty, but the park can be really dangerous," he agrees. "I've been keeping an eye on her house, and there's still no sign of her mom. Will it be OK if she stays with you?"

"I don't know," I answer truthfully. "My mother and I aren't on the best terms right now, but I can't see her turning Clara away."

"Good," he answers. "She must be a great mom to raise you and your brother so well on her own."

My guard goes up. Again, he seems to know more about me than he should. Time for some honest talk. "OK," I say. "I need to know how you know so much about me. We barely know each other, and I don't have the first clue about your life, but you seem pretty familiar with mine. Why?" I stare at him, challenging him to lie. To my great relief, he doesn't.

"Sorry," he smiles, his cheeks turning a little red. "To be perfectly honest, I've—God, how can I say this and not sound like a total idiot? I've had a bit of a crush on you for a while..." He's starting to look really uncomfortable. "So, Clara and I see each other in the neighbourhood and sometimes we hang out on the porch just talking. I knew she worked with you, so sometimes I'd ask her questions about you. She had no idea, honestly—you know how she just talks sometimes. I didn't mean to creep you out, really. You must think I'm some sort of stalker. I'll just go now, OK?" He starts to get up and I put my hand on his arm to stop him.

"No, wait," I say. "Sit down." He does, still looking like he wants to crawl into the earth. "I don't think you're a stalker and I don't think you're a creep. Honest. I—" "But as much as I want to tell him that I have a crush on him too, I just can't. In fact, I can barely admit it to myself. I've spent too many years keeping my feelings to myself, and since Mom's probably never going to speak to me again after the last time I 'expressed myself', I decide to go for the safe response. "I'm glad you're here. I don't think I could handle this situation with Clara by myself."

Maybe it's not what he's looking for, but he looks relieved anyway. "All right," he says. "We have Clara taken care of—what about Lindsay?"

"Clara says the social worker put her in a foster home, so she's safe for now."

"Well, I guess foster care is better than nothing," Danny replies, "although she'd be better off with Clara."

"I know, but how's Clara going to manage it? And I thought I had problems!"

"What kind of problems do you have?" he asks, smiling. I realize with a sensation like an electrical current going up my arm that he's moved his hand across the table so that it's just barely touching mine. I don't pull away, I freeze. Even my breathing stops for a second. Then I notice the big mall clock over his shoulder.

"Oh, damn, I have to get back to work. Sorry, but Chrissie will have a fit if I'm late coming back from break."

"No problem," Danny says. "I'll see you tomorrow at school, right? So take Clara home tonight, and we can talk about this more at lunch."

As I walk away, I can still feel a tingle from the spot where his hand touched mine. It takes a while to fade.

After work, I get Clara on the bus, despite her feeble protests. It's a bit of a struggle—she has two huge duffel bags and a knapsack with all her stuff in them, but between the two of us, we manage. When we go in the house, Mom is watching TV in the dark. Chris must already be in bed.

"Uh, Mom?" I say tentatively.

She turns around in the half-light, her face looking haggard in the flickering of the television. Again, I feel a terrible sense of guilt.

"Mm-hmm?" she answers. At least she's kind of talking to me, if that can be considered talking.

"You remember my friend Clara? She's going to stay here tonight, OK?"

"Mmm," Mom answers, and turns back to the television. I think I would almost have preferred an argument, or at least some questions, but her eyes are fixed on the screen as though it's the most important thing she could be doing.

I shrug and turn to Clara. "Let's grab your stuff then, and go up. You can have the guest room — it's not very big, and a little drafty, but everyone says the bed is comfortable."

"I'm just happy to have a bed," Clara whispers as we haul her stuff up the stairs, her eyes welling up again. "This is really awesome of you, Cass. You have no idea—"

"Don't even worry about it, okay? Really it's no trouble — there's lots of room, and I wouldn't sleep knowing you were in the park anyway, so really, you're doing me the favour." I look over my shoulder and smile at her and she grins weakly back.

"Yeah," she replies, "the park was pretty awful. God, you've got a beautiful house. Have you always lived here?"

"All my life," I answer. "It's been in our family for generations." Clara was right — it was a gorgeous house, even if it's been badly neglected since Dad died. Mom and Dad did a lot of work to it over the years, restoring the original woodwork, refinishing the hardwood floors, picking out 'period' furniture, and choosing historically accurate colours. I've never seen Dad more proud than the day the local Heritage Society presented him and mom with a plaque for all their efforts. Now, of course, the paint is peeling in places, and the roof needs work. Unfortunately, food on the table and a working furnace are the priorities when money's so tight.

"Here you are," I say, putting down her bag. "You can have the turret room."

"Oh my God, this is so cool!" Clara exclaims, looking around in amazement. "I've never been in an actual turret before — it's like a castle or something!" She sits down on the bed and sags. "I am so-o-o exhausted."

"I know," I answer. "Why don't you get some sleep and we can talk in the morning about what to do next. The bathroom is down the hall on the left. I'll grab you some towels."

After getting Clara settled, I decide that I better follow up with Mom. It could be a few days before Clara can find somewhere else to stay, and after what she's been through, I don't want her to feel like an unwelcome guest. I go back downstairs. Mom is still sitting on the couch, staring at the TV. I sit down beside her, but she doesn't acknowledge me. My stomach knots up and I clear my throat.

"Um, Mom?" I venture tentatively. She looks at me, expressionless.

"About Clara..." I continue. She's not doing anything to make me feel more at ease, but I don't really blame her, I suppose.

"What about Clara?" she finally asks after a long silence.

"Well, it's just that... she needs to stay here for a few days." I have no idea how she's going to react to this—I've never had a friend stay over even one night, let alone take up residence in the guest room. Mom reaches for the remote and mutes the TV.

"Why does Clara need to stay here for a few days?" she asks, her eyes narrowing suspiciously. I take a deep breath, then give her an abbreviated version of what happened.

Her eyes widen. "So she has nowhere else to go?"

"No—her mom told her to never come back, and she doesn't have any other family around here. I know it's a lot to ask, but can she please stay here, just for a little while until she gets things figured out?"

Mom sighs. "Cass, you're just as much a contributor to this household as I am. You don't really need my permission. If you want your friend to stay here, that's your decision, not mine." She looks back at the TV and turns the volume up again, as if the conversation is over. I can't take this—she looks so unhappy, and I know that I'm miserable. I reach over, grab the remote, and mute the TV again.

"Mom, listen," I start. She stares at me and sighs again. "I'm really sorry for what I said last night. It was a terrible thing to say and I didn't mean it." That, of course, is not entirely true. I did mean it, at least at the time, but I should have found a better way to tell her how used I felt. There's a long pause, and she finally replies. I brace myself for impact but it's not what I expect.

"Yes, it was a terrible thing to say, but you were right, Cass. I've given it a lot of thought, and I don't blame you for being angry. You've sacrificed a lot for our family, and I should have been honest with you. I lied and it was wrong. I just wish you'd said something sooner about the way you were feeling. I thought you felt like you could tell me anything, but I understand now why you're having a hard time trusting me. I'm the one who should be sorry. And I am." Her eyes start to tear up again. I put my arms around her and we hug. She sniffles, then pulls away, wipes her eyes, and smiles at me.

All this talk about lying and honesty has me feeling even worse, like the biggest hypocrite on the planet. She's probably never going to believe another word I say ever again, but I can't be angry at her for lying if I'm guilty of the same thing. "I do trust you, Mom, but sometimes it's hard for me to say what I feel. I want you to trust me too, so I have to tell you the truth about something."

She looks at me questioningly. As calmly as I can, I tell her about what happened at the party, all of it, all the gory details. When I get to the part where Tommy has me cornered, I start to cry despite myself, and she grabs my hand and squeezes it hard. She doesn't ease up until the point where Danny comes to my rescue and Tommy takes off.

"So that's why I buried the sweater," I finish. "I'm really sorry about that, but I just wasn't thinking straight. And please don't blame Clara for any of it—she's had a lousy time lately, and she knows she screwed up."

"God, sweetheart," she says. "I wish you'd told me before now. I feel like the worst mother on the planet, thinking everything was fine, when you've been so miserable."

"I just felt so stupid, Mom. Telling you about it would have meant admitting that I'm not as responsible as everyone thinks I am. But at least it worked out all right in the end. And Tommy hasn't bothered me since." Which also isn't exactly true, but the name calling was a minor thing—better to leave that detail out.

"Well," she says, "I'll tell you this much. If I ever see that jerk Tommy, I'll—knock his block off!" She raises her fist menacingly in the air.

I giggle at her old-fashioned expression, and she says, "Buried the sweater? Seriously?"

I stop laughing. "In the backyard, yeah. I couldn't look at it anymore. It was like a reminder of something awful that I'd rather not think about."

"Well, don't worry about it anymore. And just think—maybe in a thousand years, someone will dig it up as an ancient artefact and display it in a museum!"

We both laugh at that, and suddenly things seem back to normal. Then I remember Grant, and the feeling fades a little. As if she can read my mind, she says, "So are we still OK for dinner tomorrow? Grant's really looking forward to meeting you and Chris. You'll give him a chance, won't you, Cass?"

I avoid answering her question by asking, "Is it OK if Clara comes with us? I wouldn't feel right going off and leaving her alone here."

"I don't see why not," Mom answers. "Now, go to bed—you have school tomorrow. I love you, Cass."

"I love you, too. Goodnight." For the first time in a while, I feel like maybe I'll be able to get a good night's sleep.

Chapter 7

I hate getting up in the morning. My personal vision of hell is a place where alarm clocks ring constantly. This morning is no different — when the alarm goes off, I hit snooze right away, and bury my head under the covers for a few more blissful moments. Then I remember Clara, and the events of yesterday, and decide there's no point trying to go back to sleep. I get up and quietly go down the hall towards her room. There's no sign of her stirring yet. I can hear faint noises from the kitchen which means Mom's done in the bathroom so I decide to get cleaned up and ready for school instead of eating breakfast first, so I can be out of Clara's way when she wakes up.

I take a nice, hot shower, but I forget to put on the fan, so when I get out, the room is full of steam. I make my way through the mist to the mirror and wipe the condensation away. I can barely see myself — just a vague sense of blurred colour. As the room starts to clear, my reflection becomes more defined, until there I am. I've never thought I was anything special — Dad used to call me 'beautiful' all the time, but he was biased, naturally. And once, I overheard the guidance secretary refer to me as 'the pretty dark-haired girl who wants to be an archaeologist' to another staff member, but I never give much thought to my looks. I wonder what Danny thinks. He said he had a crush on me, so he must think I'm all right. Does he see me as beautiful? Personally, I think I'm kind of boring-looking—maybe I should spice it up a little. I never wear any makeup, aside from lip gloss, and I sure don't want to look like some of the girls at school who paint it on in layers, but maybe a little eye liner wouldn't hurt. I hunt around in the vanity until I find Mom's makeup bag, and pull out a tube of liquid eyeliner. I have no idea how to do this, but if Mom can use it, how hard can it be? I think about how Clara does her eyes, and start drawing. Within 10 seconds, I realize that I am nowhere near as coordinated as I thought I was. In fact, I am now a bit of a mess. There's a black line zigzagging across my upper eyelid, a black smudge under my eyebrow, and as I take my hand away, I graze my cheek with the wand. Great. Well, I don't look boring anymore, just insane. I grab a washcloth and start scrubbing. Big mistake—the more I scrub, the more the eyeliner just gets spread around, and now the side of my face is one big, black smear. How am I going to go to school looking like this? Suddenly, there's a knock at the door, and I hear Clara's voice.

"Cass? Are you in there?"

I open the door, and she immediately bursts out laughing. "What on earth are you doing?!" she gasps.

"It's eyeliner. How the hell do you get this stuff off?!" I'm more than a little embarrassed at this point, but if she has any make-up removal advice, I'll be happy to take it.

"Oh, no problem," she says. "If you don't have eye makeup remover, you can use moisturizer and a cotton ball. Just be careful not to get any in your eye." She starts laughing again. "God, Cass, you should have just asked me to do it for you. So who's the guy you're trying to impress?"

"What? Oh, no guy." I'm not ready to discuss Danny with anyone yet. The moisturizer is doing the trick, and I start looking like myself again. I decide that Danny is going to have to take me the way he finds me. "There, that's better," I say. "Thanks for the help. So, what's your plan for today?"

"Well," Clara says thoughtfully, leaning against the doorjamb, "I decided last night that my immediate problem is money. So I thought today I'd go to the mall, and ask Jim if I could start working at You Jane full-time. And if not, then I'd see who else is hiring. Maybe I can pick up extra hours somewhere else. I'd been saving money for college, and I have enough right now to use for a rent deposit, but I need a bigger, steady income to afford an apartment for Lindsay and me. Then I'm going to see the social worker who put Lindsay in the foster home, and find out what I need to do to get her back."

"What about your mom?" I ask. "Won't she want Lindsay back?"

Clara laughs cynically. "Seriously, Cass, all my mom cares about is whatever guy is supplying her with booze and drugs. She's probably thrilled to get rid of both of us. After everything that's happened, there's no way I'd let her have custody of Lindsay."

"Well, it sounds like a good plan anyway. I'm sure Jim will be able to find you some more hours. And if not, I hear that Mexicana Deluxe is hiring," I joke. She grimaces. "So have a good day, and I'll see you later. Text me if you need anything. Oh, by the way, can you be back by 5? We're all going out for dinner tonight and you're invited."

"Oh..." Her cheeks flush a little and she looks uncomfortable. "That sounds great, but I don't really have a lot of money right now. I should probably pass. In fact, can I borrow some money for bus fare? Just until I can get to the mall and go to the bank? I'll pay you back, I promise."

"Of course. But don't worry about dinner—it's on me. I owe you for helping me get that goop off my face—no arguments," I say firmly, as she starts to protest. "Besides, I need a buffer tonight—my mom is introducing us to her new boyfriend." Her eyebrows shoot up at this revelation, but I take off downstairs before she can ask any questions. "I'll leave the bus fare on the table by the front door," I yell back up the stairs, then go in the kitchen for breakfast.

I walk in the room and I'm met with a chorus of "Surprise!" and "Happy Birthday!" Chris launches himself at me and wraps his arms around me, singing "It's your birthday, it's your birthday!" in an excited, breathless voice. Mom is standing by the stove, spatula in hand, beaming.

"One special pancake breakfast for my birthday girl," she says, as she comes over and kisses me on the cheek. "I can't believe you're seventeen already," she sighs. "It seems like only yesterday, you were wearing Care Bear pyjamas and begging your dad for 'one more story'. Do you remember that? Every night—'one more story, Daddy, just one more!' And he would always say—"

"—'One more?! Are you craaaaa-zzyy?!' And then he would read it anyway," I finish. I always miss him a little bit more on special occasions. It seems so unfair that he can't be there to celebrate with us. Some of the brightness goes out of my day as I remember the way I could hear his voice as I was drifting off to sleep, the last thing I heard every night. It was so comforting. He read to me from the time I was old enough to sit up—even when I got older, he would always read at least one chapter of a book to me at bedtime, especially after Chris was born and Mom was so busy taking care of him. And even when Dad got sick, he kept reading to me every night—as the cancer got worse, his voice got weaker, until it was barely a whisper, and he could hardly hold the book in his hands. Still, he read to me until he was admitted into the hospital. And then I read to him. I don't want to think about this anymore, not with Mom and Chris staring at me expectantly, big grins on their faces, so I smile and say, "So where are these famous pancakes?"

"Here you go, honey." Mom puts down a plate with a stack of pancakes and maple syrup, topped with a lit candle.

"Make a wish, Cass, make a wish!" Chris is jumping up and down. "Wait 'til you see what I got you for your birthday!"

"Yes," Mom says, "we thought it might be a good idea to give you your presents this morning instead of at the restaurant. Chris was a little too excited to wait."

I blow out the candle. I don't bother making a wish, because it wouldn't come true anyway. As I start digging into the mound of pancakes, Chris reaches under the table and brings out a misshapen package. He puts it in front of me and whispers, "I wrapped it myself."

"Really?" I reply, trying not to laugh at the huge amount of tape he apparently used. "Great job!"

"You can open it now," he orders. When I finally release it from all the tape and paper, I'm not quite sure what it is. It's a pottery lump, glazed in green, with spikes and something that looks like a stubby tail.

"This is awesome, Chris... I... obviously it's..."

"The Almighty Rat! I made it myself in art. It's made out of clay. I never used clay before, but I think it looks pretty good. Do you like it?"

"I love it," I answer. "It's really unique."

As Chris continues telling me all about the kiln and the glazes, Mom slips an envelope over to me. I open it and it's a birthday card. Inside is a gift card to the mall.

"I thought maybe you could buy yourself something nice. Maybe a new sweater." She winks and I smile back. Considering how different our tastes are, it's actually a pretty thoughtful gift. The last time she bought me clothes for my birthday, I was fourteen, and it was a bright, red blouse with a lace collar. I only wore it once, to dinner that night, and I remember cringing when she told me how 'lovely' I looked.

"Thanks, Mom," I say. "I can't wait to go shopping. And I love my Rat." I put my arm around Chris and kiss him on top of the head. "C'mon you—let's get ready for school."

Mom leaves for work, and Chris and I get dressed. It's easier now that he's older and needs less help. All I really have to do is make sure that his clothes kind of match (and that he's not wearing his Ratsuit), and that he brushes his teeth, which he hates to do. I walk him to the corner where the crossing guard is waiting, then we go our separate ways.

When I walk down the hall at school towards my locker, I realize that Danny is already there, waiting for me. My heart kind of jumps and I have to remind myself to stay cool.

"Hi," I say, as I nonchalantly drop my knapsack and start to open my locker. For some bizarre reason, I can't seem to remember the combination. I just keep twirling the dial around, getting more flustered with each passing second. The fact that he smells good isn't helping my concentration.

"Hi," Danny smiles back. "Are you having a problem with your lock?"

It suddenly snaps open. "Nope, no problem," I answer. "So... how are things?" I'm not very good at small talk, obviously.

"Fine," he answers. "How's Clara doing?"

At least now I have something specific to talk about. I fill him in on her plan for the day. "I hope Jim can give her some extra hours," I finish.

"Well, it sounds like a good place to start," he replies. "I have an update too." I look at him quizzically and he continues. "When I got home yesterday, Clara's car was back in the driveway. After a little while, another car pulled up and this guy got out. He had a For Rent sign and he started hammering it into the lawn. All of a sudden, the door opened, and Clara's mom came staggering out—I mean, really staggering, obviously wasted. She started screaming at the guy, and he started yelling back. What I got from the argument was that she was already 3 months behind on rent, and having the police there was the last straw. He told her she had until Saturday morning to clear out, and then he was having the locks changed. When I left for school this morning, the car was gone again."

"Wow." I don't know what else to say.

"I know, it's crazy, right? I mean, we lived down the street from them for over 2 years now, and I would never have guessed anything like this would happen. Just goes to show that you never know what other people's lives are like."

"Well," I say, "maybe it's a good thing that her mom's gone. That way Clara won't have to worry about getting custody of Lindsay if there's no one else around."

"True," Danny replies. "I'm so glad my parents are relatively normal. They can be weird sometimes—my dad likes to sing opera in public, and my mom hides her eyes every time I take a hit at a tournament, but they love me."

We both laugh. I say, "Every time you take a hit?"

"Luckily, I don't get hit that much, or she'd never see any of my bouts. Speaking of which..." He pauses, and I look at him expectantly. He clears his throat. "So, there's that tournament this weekend, Sunday, the one Miles and I were talking about. I was wondering if you wanted to come and watch. Then maybe after, we could get a bite to eat or see a movie or something."

My ears can hardly believe what they're hearing. I've never been asked out on a date before—well, at least not by anyone I wanted to go out with. He looks away, puts his hands in his pockets, and says, "If you're busy or some-thing—"

"No! I mean, I'm not busy. That sounds like fun." We both relax, and I say, "I'll have to check with my mom, but I'm sure it won't be a problem. I don't know about watching you get hit though."

He laughs. "It's just an intercity tournament, nothing to worry about. It'll be fun, I promise. We should probably get to class now — keep me posted if you hear anything from Clara."

"I will. I—I should probably give you my cell number," I say hesitantly, then think of a good excuse. "Just in case anything else happens at Clara's house."

"Oh, good idea!" he says, playing along. "I'll give you mine too — just in case."

As we're exchanging numbers, Tara and Megan walk by. They elbow each other and stare, then smirk knowingly at me. I ignore them. They're so annoying, and God knows what they're telling people about me, but the truth is, I really don't care. I have a date.

Chapter 8

When I get home after school, Clara's already there, looking like she's about to burst.

"Oh my God, Cass—what a day!" she says, before I even put my knapsack down.

"So what did you find out? You seem pretty excited." I hope she had some success today, before I have to tell her about her mom and really bring her down.

"Well, first of all, I talked to Jim. He said I came at just the right time, because he's looking for an assistant manager. I guess Chrissie is finding it too hard to juggle university classes with work and she wants to cut back on her hours!"

"Chrissie goes to university?" I have to admit I'm a little shocked.

"I know, right? Who would have guessed! At any rate, he gave me the job right then and there—I start on Monday. And he said that in September, Chrissie would probably give up working at You Jane altogether, so if I worked out as assistant manager, I could have her manager's job then!"

"Clara, that's really awesome news. Did you get a chance to talk to the social worker?"

Her face clouds over a little. "Yes, she filled me in on a couple of things. The good news is that if I can prove I have a steady income and a place to live, then I can get guardianship of Lindsay, at least if mom doesn't fight it, but the social worker said she hadn't been able to get in touch with mom yet and didn't know where she was. The bad news is that Frank is out on bail, even though he has a record. She wouldn't tell me what he'd done, and I don't even want to guess. Anyway, she said to be careful, and to call the cops if he came anywhere near me. But he doesn't know where I am, so I'm not too worried." Her face brightened. "Do you get the local paper? I can't wait to start looking for an apartment!"

"Yeah, it should be here any minute. So, I have some news about your mom—I don't know if it's good news or bad news though." I fill her in on what Danny told me earlier. "Is there anything in the house that you want? If there is, we better get it before Saturday."

Clara looks upset. "Not much—just some books and a couple of pictures of me and Lindsay when we were little. I'm just really mad about the car, if you want to know the truth. It's my car, I saved up to buy it, and it's registered to me. She has no right to be driving it around like she owns it."

"You could talk to the police, have them look for it or something," I suggest.

"Not a chance. If they find the car, then they might find her, and I really want her to stay gone. I guess I'll just have to cut my losses."

At this, the door flies open and Chris and Nolan run in. Nolan has the newspaper and he's whacking Chris over the head with it. Chris is laughing, but I yell, "Hey, take it easy, kid!" Nolan is distracted for a second—Chris takes advantage by grabbing the paper out of his hand, and giving him a whack in return. Then he drops it and they both run through the house and out to the back yard.

"Well, here's the newspaper anyway." I hand it to Clara. "Why don't you take a look at the rentals while I make the boys a snack?" She takes the paper eagerly and goes into the living room. I'm anxious to see what she finds. Not that I mind having Clara around, but it would be great for her to get her life back on track.

When I'm done fixing PB and J sandwiches for Chris and Nolan (no 'J' for Nolan because "jam is gross"), I go back into the living room. The paper is lying on the floor, and Clara looks despondent.

"What's wrong," I ask. "Isn't there anything available?"

"Oh no, there's lots available. They're just too expensive! There isn't a single place I could afford and still be able to eat every day. What am I going to do?"

I don't know what to say to her. "We'll figure something out, Clara, don't worry. Maybe my mom will have some ideas. We can talk to her later about it. Keep looking—maybe you missed something."

"Okay," she sighs. "I'm just going to stay here and think. Don't worry about me—just go do your thing. What time are we leaving for dinner?"

"In about an hour, when my mom gets home. I should start getting Chris ready—it takes him forever to do anything."

"Oh, wait a minute!" Clara says. "Don't go anywhere!" She races out of the room. When she comes back, she's holding a gift-wrapped box. "Happy Birthday!" she says. "I saw the birthday cards and the pancake with the candle on it, and I couldn't resist getting you this."

"Oh, Clara, that's really sweet—you didn't have to get me anything." I feel terribly guilty, especially since I know how worried about money she is.

"Well, you've been so great about everything, letting me stay here, and helping me, that I wanted to do something for you. I hope you like it."

I tear off the paper. It's a make-up kit—blush, eye shadow, mascara, and of course, the dreaded eyeliner. We both laugh.

"I thought you could use it to practice with before you ever go out in public with eyeliner on!"

"That's really thoughtful, Clara—thanks. Although it'll be ages before I'm skilled enough to wear this stuff outside of the house." But, I think to myself, maybe if I practice really hard, I'll be ready to wear it on Sunday.

♦ ♦ ♦

I have to admit that I'm really upset. Here's why:

1) The Golden Dragon is my favourite restaurant in the world. We've been coming here for years, mainly because Dad loved Chinese food, and because of that, so did I. And not just the food. The Golden Dragon is decorated like a Chinese pagoda, with red and gold lanterns and statues and paintings on the walls of Chinese scenes. But the best part is the fish. There's a huge tank by the entrance filled with gigantic koi fish. Dad and I named them when I was little, and every time we came here, we would greet all the fish by name. It was a tradition to stand in front of the tank and say, "Hello, Harvey, hello Jacques, hello Miss Bubbles", and so on. Koi live for years, so it was always the same fish. They were like old friends. The Golden Dragon is a special place.

2) My father is dead. He can no longer enjoy The Golden Dragon with me, nor can he greet the fish with me.

3) I have been taken to The Golden Dragon, a special place, on my birthday, to meet my mom's new boyfriend

I'm trying very hard to smile. Grant is meeting us at the restaurant. We've already arrived, and are sitting at the table, waiting. Mom keeps talking nervously about nothing in particular, eyeing the door every 10 seconds. Chris is telling Clara all about The Amazing Rat, and she's pretending to be intensely interested. I'm pretending to pay attention to Mom, nodding and smiling in all the right places, but I'm getting more stressed out as time goes by. Then suddenly, Mom smiles wide and waves at the door. I look over and see a man coming towards us. He looks absolutely ordinary. Average height, average build, standard haircut, blue suit, white shirt, blue tie. He even has a briefcase. Yep, there's no question he works in insurance. When he gets to the table, he gives Mom a big smile and says, "Sorry I'm a little late. Traffic." He sits down and kisses her on the cheek. I haven't seen her look so happy in years. I haven't felt so miserable.

We all just stare at each other, until Mom finally breaks the ice and says, "Everyone, this is my friend, Grant. Grant, these are my children, Cassandra and Chris, and this is Cass's friend Clara. Clara is staying with us for a few days." Grant smiles knowingly. I wonder how much Mom's told him about what happened to Clara.

"I'm happy to meet you all," he says. "I've certainly heard a lot about you two from your mother. All good, of course." He laughs a little too loudly, then clears his throat and looks at Mom, who smiles at him encouragingly. I realize that he's as unsure about this as I am.

Chris says, "Do you want to see the fish? They all have names, you know."

Grant looks at Mom. "Go on, you guys," she says. "The waitress won't be here for a minute yet." Chris is already out of his chair, and Grant follows him over to the tank. As soon as they're out of earshot, Mom whispers excitedly, "So, what do you think?!"

"Mom, I just met him, I don't know. He's OK, I guess." I don't know what else to say, but she seems content with my answer. I imagine she's just happy I didn't scream and run out. I watch Grant and Chris at the fish tank. Chris is talking animatedly and pointing at all the fish, and Grant is looking at him and nodding seriously. I can't help but think that it should be Dad and Chris over there. On a rational level, I know it's not Grant's fault that Dad is dead, but it still hurts. I sigh.

"What, honey?" Mom asks.

"Nothing. I'm just hungry. Where's the waitress?" There's nothing I can do. Sometimes, life just sucks.

After dinner, which was amazing as always, life starts sucking a little less—at least for Clara. Mom suggests that we all go around the table, reading our fortunes from the fortune cookies to each other. They're pretty cheesy, as always. Mine says, 'You will step on the soil of many countries'. Mom says, "See, Cass—archaeology will take you places!" Hers says 'You will take a chance on something in the near future.' When she reads it out, she turns a little red, and Grant smiles to himself. What is that all about? I wonder. When we get to Clara, she reads out, 'You will overcome difficult times'.

"Well, that's good news, anyway," she says, folding the fortune and putting it in her pocket. "Now, if I could just find a cheap apartment, I'd be set."

"Oh," says Grant, "are you looking for somewhere to live?" He sounds innocent, but I can tell by the way Mom looks at him out of the corner of her eye that he knows more than he's letting on.

"Yeah," Clara sighs. "There's not a lot out there in my price range."

"If it's any help," he says, "I have a friend who's the manager of an apartment complex. I know he has a small one-bedroom that's just become available and the rent is really cheap—I think he said $650 a month plus utilities. I know he's hoping to find someone right away."

"You're joking!" Clara exclaims. "I could actually afford that—do you have his number?!"

Grant writes it down on the back of what looks like one of his business cards. Clara takes it and says, "Thanks so much!", then looks at me, barely able to suppress her excitement.

We all order ice cream for dessert, and when it arrives, mine has a sparkler in it. Mom says, "Happy Birthday, honey," and suddenly all the wait staff are there and everyone is singing Happy Birthday. Luckily, the sparkler is shooting its sparks in all directions, so no one can see me get teary. When they're finished and the waitresses and waiters wander away, Grant pulls a present out of his briefcase. Dear God, what new hell is this?

He says, "I know we've just met, but your mom's told me all about your plans for the future. I hope you like it."

He hands it to me and I slowly remove the wrapping. It's a book called *Ancient Civilizations and Artefacts*.

"Wow, that's great," I say, forcing a smile. "Thanks so much."

When the bill arrives, Mom reaches for it, but Grant gets there first. "No, Janine, let me. My pleasure, really."

Mom makes a half-hearted protest, then they look at each other and laugh. I look around the table. Clara is ecstatic, Chris is contentedly stabbing the table with his chopsticks and Mom and Grant are making eyes at each other. So why can't I be happy too? Grant doesn't seem that bad — there must be something wrong with me. If only I could figure out how to fix me.

The first thing Clara does when we get home is practically run for the phone. She would have used her cell by now, but the charger is still at her house and after this long, her cell battery is dead. I hear her talking breathlessly with someone, presumably Grant's friend, and after she hangs up, she comes bouncing into the kitchen where I'm putting leftovers into the refrigerator.

"I take it you have some good news," I say, smiling at her.

"Yep! I have an appointment tomorrow at one o'clock to see the place and fill in a rental application, but he said that since Grant has already given me a reference, it shouldn't be a problem and I could move in right away. He warned me that it was really small, but that's OK—it's not like I have a lot of furniture or anything." Then her face falls. "God, I didn't even think about furniture. Cass, I don't have any, not even a chair. What are Lindsay and I going to sleep on?"

"We have a couple of sleeping bags around here you could use if you want to." I pause. "But hang on—what about your bedroom furniture back at the house? I hate to sound mercenary, but who knows where your mom is? And Danny said the landlord threatened to change the locks on Saturday morning, so he'd probably just put all the stuff in the house into storage or sell it anyway." Sometimes I'm amazed at how practical I can be. Clara seems to think so too, because she starts nodding and smiling.

"Yeah, you're right," she replies enthusiastically. "Anyway, she has my car, doesn't she? It seems like a fair trade—some furniture for a car. Besides, what's she going to do with it? She'd probably just sell it for beer money. But how am I going to move it all? I don't know if I could rent a moving truck at such short notice, let alone afford one."

As we're contemplating this dilemma, Mom comes into the kitchen. "Boy, am I stuffed!" she says. "What a great meal—I wish you had a birthday every week, Cass. So what are you two doing? You both look lost in thought."

Clara explains the problem to Mom, who thinks for a minute then says, "You know, I just might have a solution. There's a cube van at work that we sometimes use to help families move things when there's a flood or a fire. I don't see why we couldn't borrow it. I'll call Grant and find out. When do you need it for?"

"Tomorrow night would be perfect, if it's possible," replies Clara. Mom goes into the other room to use the phone, and Clara turns to me with a pained look on her face. "I can't believe how great you and your family are, Cass. There's no way I could do this on my own. I owe you so much—I don't know how I'll ever be able to repay you."

"It's the least I can do for the girl who introduced me to the wonderful world of marijuana," I joke, trying to make her feel better.

"Oh don't remind me!" she cried. "I still feel awful about that."

"Well, you should, because now if I ever get elected to public office, I'll have to admit I inhaled!" We're both laughing as Mom comes back into the room.

"Grant says it's no problem to use the van tomorrow. In fact, he said he'd be happy to help with the heavy lifting! He'll be here tomorrow after work, and we can all go over then."

Clara jumps up and hugs Mom. "That's fantastic," she says. "Grant really is awesome!"

"Yeah, Grant's a peach," I say under my breath. Not quietly enough though, because Mom shoots me a sharp look over Clara's shoulder. But she doesn't say anything, so maybe she didn't hear me after all.

I clear my throat. "So anyway, it's getting late. I should get Chris ready for bed and tackle a little homework."

"I'll come up too," says Clara. "I want to make a list of all the things we should take from the house. Goodnight, Mrs. Wilson. Thanks again."

I go over and give Mom a kiss on the cheek. "And thanks for a great birthday dinner, Mom. Clara, go on ahead, I'll be right up." I need to talk to Mom about going out with Danny on Sunday, but I'm still not comfortable having other people know about it, even Clara. I tell Mom about Danny's invitation, and she looks at me with a knowing expression on her face.

"So your knight in shining armour is turning out to be more than a friend, is he? Well, I'm very happy for you — so when do I get to meet this Danny? He sounds like an interesting young man."

"Well, I was thinking of asking him if he could help out tomorrow with Clara's move. He just lives a few houses down from her, and I'm sure he wouldn't mind." To be honest, I hadn't been thinking about it until this very moment, but it is a good idea. It occurs to me that if Clara's mother has finally decided to come home, there might be some problems, and Grant doesn't look like the most aggressive guy on the planet. But I have no doubt that Danny could deal with the situation. Besides, it'll be nice to see him outside of school, where the gossip girls aren't hanging on our every move.

Chapter 9

Today is another uneventful day at school. Danny is waiting for me at my locker again, and he agrees to help move Clara's furniture without hesitation. We go our separate ways, but meet up for a quick lunch together in the cafeteria. The girls I sometimes eat with give me hurtful looks as I walk by with Danny, but I don't feel too bad—I'm pretty sure any one of them would ditch me for a guy. And besides, it's not as if we're really close. We're more like a group of people who gravitate towards each other because it's better than eating alone. In fact, I don't really know too much about any of them aside from what I've gleaned through conversations I barely listen to. Here's the extent of my knowledge: Lisa is hyper skinny, wears braces, which she hates, and wants to become a published poet. I've read her poetry, and it's all haiku, so I don't think she has much of a chance, but who am I to judge? There's Ling, who's from Hong Kong, but who lives here with her aunt and uncle so that she can take advantage of our school's academic programs. She's extremely smart, and also extremely aware that she's extremely smart. Not always a good combination. Maggie is really pretty in a cheerleader kind of way, and manages to involve herself in any school activity going. She's a vegan, and she eats with us because she got fed up with the other "Activities" kids trying to sneak lunch meat into her tofu sandwiches. We, on the other hand, respect her decision, or at least don't hassle her about it. Kim is here today—she has an on-again, off-again relationship with a guy named Kenny. When they're 'on', they eat and snuggle together in a quiet basement corridor known as the Dungeon, where kids can go and paw each other away from the eyes of the teachers on hall supervision. When they're 'off', Kim eats with us and trash talks Kenny. Finally, there's Sam, loud and lesbian. She's a member of the school's Rainbow Connection, and considers herself an activist. And while she wouldn't ditch me for a guy, she wouldn't hesitate if one of the senior Teen Queens, like Jasmine Ogilvy, batted her eyes in Sam's direction—Sam has been crushing on her for two years despite the fact that Jasmine is as straight as an arrow.

Danny and I find a table near the big bank of windows that overlooks the front lawn and the "native plants and grasses" garden that the horticultural club created—it looks pretty straggly, in my opinion, but what do I know? Our garden at home is full of perennials—Mom's attitude is "I'll plant it, but if it can't survive on its own, there's nothing I can do about it." As for me, I'm pretty handy with a hedge trimmer (did you know you can use one of those to cut grass?), but that's about it. I open my lunch bag, and take out a ham sandwich, yogurt, and a banana. In the meantime, Danny hoists his backpack onto the table, and starts pulling out container after container. I've never seen anything like it—what looks like a cold half-chicken, three sandwiches, a bag of carrots, two thermoses... it's never-ending. I can't help but ask.

"Are you really going to eat all that?!"

Danny laughs and opens up one of the thermoses, which looks like it's full of hot pasta. "I have to meet my weigh-in target for Sunday's tournament. And the way I've been training lately, I need to replenish my proteins and carbs like crazy. Are you planning on eating that banana?"

"No, you go ahead," I say, passing it to him with a bemused look on my face. He starts shovelling in the pasta with one hand and takes the banana with the other. "What's in the other thermos?" I ask.

"Protein shake," he manages to get out between spoonfuls. "By the way, I won't be at school this afternoon. I'm meeting with my trainer to go over some last minute strategy — just refining everything, you know? But I'll be at Clara's by 6:00 at the latest to help."

"Great," I sigh. "It'll be good to get her stuff out so that she can have a fresh start." He nods, his mouth full, and we sit in comfortable silence for a while, finishing our lunches. Surprisingly, and despite all the food he had, he's done not long after me.

"Wow," he says, "I don't think I could eat anything else right now."

I raise my eyebrows. "I hate to tell you this, but there *isn't* anything else!" We both laugh, and start to pack up. "I have to get to chemistry a bit early to set up a lab," I say, standing up.

He stands up too, and comes around my side of the table. "No problem," he says. "I better head out too. See you at Clara's." And then he kisses me on the cheek, throws his backpack over his shoulder and leaves. Just like that. Like it was the most normal thing in the world. I'm immobilized. I've never actually been kissed by a boy before. Well, all right, there was Billy Kimmel in second grade, who would chase the girls, and if he caught you, he'd plant a disgustingly sloppy kiss on you anywhere he could. But this was different. I feel myself getting red, then a smile spreads over my face, and I decide I've better start moving before anyone wonders why this strange, happy girl is standing frozen in the middle of the cafeteria.

◆ ◆ ◆

The situation with Tommy Fillmore has taken a disturbing and unpleasant turn. I'm pretty shaken up, but I don't know what to do. I'm afraid to tell Danny, but things are really getting out of hand and I don't think I can ignore it anymore. This afternoon was beautiful, warm and sunny — the kind of weather where you just want to lie flat on the grass with your eyes closed and daydream. I guess I wasn't the only one who felt that way, because half-way through fourth period, out of the blue, the fire alarm went off. It was pretty obvious that it wasn't a planned fire drill — teachers were giving each other 'the look' in the hallway, that kind of panicky look that asks silently, "Did you know about this? Were we told? It's not a real fire, is it!?" As for us, there was an undercurrent of excitement, the thrill of getting out of class and into the sunshine, if only for a little while. I remember that I was standing on the back lawn with the rest of my class, but a little away from everybody, lost in my own world, still thinking about Danny and wondering about the kiss on the cheek — did that mean he considered us a 'couple'? — when out of the blue, I was hit from behind so hard that I flew forward and my binders hit the ground, the papers scattering everywhere. As I looked around wildly, trying to figure out what had just happened, I realized that Tommy was standing there with his hands in his pockets, watching me with a smug, satisfied look on his face.

I started to get really angry and was just about to tell him off when he said with a sneer, just quietly enough that no one else could hear, "You're not so tough when your boyfriend's not around, huh? You slut." Then he turned and walked away, leaving me there with my mouth hanging open in shock, surrounded by binders and papers. By this time, a couple of girls from my class, Carla Jamison and Lisa Singh, had made their way over and had started to help me pick everything up.

"What happened, Cass?" Carla asked, handing me a sheath of papers.

"Yeah, are you OK?" Lisa followed up. "You look a little pale. What did Tommy say to you?"

"Oh, he just asked if I needed help. God, I'm so clumsy," I lied, trying to laugh, but I really wanted to throw up.

We finished picking everything up. Carla smiled sympathetically and said, "Maybe you should go home—you don't look so well."

"Yeah, maybe," I answered. "Thanks for your help. Now I just need to put all these papers back in order." I hope my smile wasn't too fake, and that they didn't notice my hands shaking. I did come home early; I told the secretary in the main office that I was feeling sick, which wasn't a lie. I'm really at a loss here—if I tell Danny, I don't know how he'll react, and I don't want him to get into trouble on my account. But at the same time, I can't let things go on like this. I actually have a bruise on my back from where Tommy body checked me. I need to pull myself together. It's already 4:30 pm. Mom and Grant will be here anytime with the cube van, and I don't want anyone to see me like this, especially Danny. I managed to get Chris a snack without him noticing that there was anything wrong, but he's too young to really tell when people are faking it. Mom, on the other hand, is a lot more perceptive. And I refuse to let what happened with Tommy spoil my time with Danny later. I decide for now to just stay out of Tommy's way and keep my eyes open for sneak attacks. He doesn't have a very big attention span anyway, from what I can see, so hopefully he'll get bored soon and leave me alone.

Chapter 10

I manage to pull myself together just as Clara comes bouncing into the house. I mean literally bouncing — she's so happy that she's jumping up and down with excitement.

"Cass, it's so amazing! The apartment is perfect, just the right size for Lindsay and me. Jeff, the landlord, said I can move in tonight, no problem. I already called your Mom at work and told her, so we're good to go with the van. First thing tomorrow, I'm going to call the social worker and get Lindsay back. She can't say no — there's a really good school two blocks away that Lindsay can go to. Plus, there's a lady who lives across from the building who runs a home daycare — I already talked to her about taking care of Lindsay after school until I get home from work."

"That's fantastic, Clara," I say, meaning it. "Mom and Grant should be here any minute — have you got everything packed?"

"Crap! I totally forgot about doing that. It won't take very long though — I don't have that much stuff."

I start to laugh. "Not that much? I still remember trying to lug one of those duffel bags on and off the bus. It weighed a ton!"

Clara's face falls and she sighs. "I know. You were such a big help that night. I don't know what I would have done without you. You know, I'm really happy to be moving on, but I'll miss being here. You have an amazing family, Cass. There aren't too many people who would have made a stranger feel so welcome." She gives me a hug and I hug her back. I'm actually going to miss her too. Having her around was almost like having an older sister. An older sister whose life was full of messy drama, but still...

"You're not a stranger, you're a friend. And we'll all miss you too. Now go get your stuff packed—do you need help?"

"No, I'm good," she says, and heads for the stairs. "I'll be down in a minute!"

Sure enough, it's not long before she's dragging her earthly possessions down the stairs, just as Mom pulls in, with Grant in the van right behind her. I watch through the window as Mom gets out of the car and heads back to where Grant is. They stand in the driveway talking and laughing for a minute. At one point, Grant reaches out and tucks a stray piece of Mom's hair behind her ear, and she smiles up at him the way I remember her smiling at Dad. My heart lurches. I guess I just don't understand how you can love one person for so long, then start to love someone else in the exact same way. And she does love him—I can tell.

Then they come in the house, and I'm distracted by the ensuing chaos. Clara is trying, not very successfully, to stack her bags in the hall, Chris is yelling about riding in the van with Grant, and Mom is generally fussing over Clara, making sure that she hasn't forgotten anything. Grant and I make eye contact and he smiles at me. I try to smile back— I'm sure he has no idea how I feel, and he seems like a great guy, but it's so hard. Instead, I grab Clara's backpack and call out over the din, "We should load up and get going! It's getting close to 6 o'clock!"

When we arrive at Clara's old house, Danny is sitting on the front porch waiting for us. I'm surprised to see that his hair isn't green anymore, it's more of an ash blond, and instead of being spiked straight up, it's casually brushed back and to one side. I had no problem with the green hair, but I have to admit, he looks even better than usual. As he walks over, I look at him questioningly. He leans over and whispers, "I didn't want to freak out your mom. Besides, it was time for a change anyway."

I introduce Danny to Mom, Grant, and Chris, who immediately asks, "Do you like the Almighty Rat?"

Danny replies, in the same bizarre voice that Chris uses, "Ah, yes. Almighty Rat is great fighter. Knows much kung fu." Chris giggles and Mom give me a subtle look of approval. In the meantime, Clara has retrieved the key to the house from under a rock next to the porch and has opened the front door. As I go past her, she smiles and nods towards Danny, and says, "I think there's something you've been keeping from me. We definitely have to talk later."

I start to blush. I'd kind of forgotten that I hadn't said anything to Clara about Danny. Well, the cat's out of the bag now, so to speak.

Danny and Grant come over, and Grant asks, "Where should we start?"

We all go into the house to start moving out the bigger pieces of furniture that Clara has put on the list. We're in the process of loading the bed into the van, when suddenly a car pulls up and a very angry-looking man comes storming across the front lawn. Clara looks frightened.

"It's our landlord, Mr. Vanelli. God, what does he want?"

Grant moves in to intercept Mr. Vanelli before he gets to Clara. Danny, likewise, plants himself between the angry landlord and the rest of us.

"What's going on here?!" Vanelli shouts at us. "What do you think you're doing?!"

Grant answers calmly, "We're moving out this young lady's furniture. What seems to be the problem?"

"The problem?!" yells Vanelli. "The problem is that I'm owed 3 months' rent, and no one is taking anything out of this house until I get it!"

"Hang on just a minute!" Mom starts to come forward, sounding concerned, but Grant puts his hand up, gives her a knowing smile, and she stops.

"Well," says Grant, turning back to the landlord. His voice seems soothing, but there's an edge under it. "I can see you're upset. But let me explain a couple of things to you." Vanelli stops yelling and looks uncertainly at Grant, who continues. "First, this young lady isn't the leaseholder—she doesn't owe you any money, her mother does, and no one knows where her mother is. Second, she is an innocent victim of circumstance, and I think anyone would agree that it would be wrong to deny her the furniture she needs to make a new start for herself and her sister. And third, we're happy to leave enough of the contents for you to either sell or keep. You could advertise the house as 'partially furnished' if you'd like."

Vanelli seems to calm down. He looks speculatively at the furniture in the truck—a bed, a dresser, a pull-out couch, a table and chairs, lamps, and a few other odds and ends. Finally, he grunts. "All right. But make sure you leave the TV and the stereo. At least I can get something out of this mess."

Clara sighs. "Fair enough, Mr. Vanelli. I'll be too exhausted for the next little while to even think about watching TV anyway. Thanks for letting me take all of this." She gestures to the truck. Vanelli grunts again. She says, "I'll give you my new address, just in case there's anything in the house you decide you don't want." She writes it on a piece of paper, which he crumples and shoves it into his pocket.

"Just hurry up and clear out. I got people coming by later to look at the place." With that, he goes back to his car and drives away.

Clara turns to Grant. "Thank you so much! That guy scares the pants off me. If you hadn't been here—"

"No problem," Grant replies with a grin. "I have to deal with people like him quite often in my business. I find the best thing is just to keep calm and act like you know what you're talking about!" Everyone laughs, me included, and I notice Danny relaxing. He had looked ready to spring into action the entire time that Mr. Vanelli was here.

We manage to finish up in good time, and head over to Clara's new apartment, where the unloading process begins. I'm kind of glad at this point that she didn't take much from the house—my back and arms are getting sore and tired from all the lifting and carrying. Danny and Chris seem to be getting along really well though. They spend the entire time laughing, joking, and karate chopping each other in between loads, which has Chris as happy as I've ever seen him. When the big pieces of furniture are in place, Danny comes over to where I'm standing by the truck and says, "Your little brother is great."

"I know," I reply. "You know, it never occurred to me until now how much he must miss doing 'guy stuff' with someone older and more mature. Although the way you keep talking in that Ratman voice, I'm starting to wonder about the 'mature'." I laugh and mock-elbow him.

"Hey!" he protests, and mock-elbows me back. We smile at each other until Chris interrupts.

"Come on, Danny! I want to show you this really cool move I invented!"

Danny replies, "Okay, partner," but Mom interjects.

"Slow down, Chris—you're going to wear Danny out. And besides, the pizza is on its way."

Chris, easily distracted by the thought of pizza, yells "All right! I want pepperoni!" and runs into the apartment.

Clara's new place is really small, but it's clean, and just right for her and Lindsay. Clara sets up the bedroom for her little sister and declares that she's happy sleeping on the pull-out couch in the living room so that Lindsay can have a room of her own. The pizza arrives and we all just sit in a circle on the floor, munching away happily. Clara is ecstatic—you can tell by the way she's talking about how she's going to decorate Lindsay's room, and how the social worker will have no choice but to give her guardianship, and how she'll want to meet Lindsay's new teacher; she's barely paying any attention to the slice of pizza in her hand. The rest of us listen in comfortable and happy silence, agreeing with her in between bites. Suddenly, she exclaims, "My cell phone!" and jumps up. She starts rummaging through a box and pulls out her charger.

"Finally, I can charge the darn thing!" She goes into the kitchen and starts looking for an electrical outlet to plug it into. Mom takes advantage of her absence, and the silence it brings, by turning to Danny.

"So," she says. "Cass tells me that you're really into martial arts—kung fu and kickboxing, right?" I start praying that she's not going to get all 'mother hen' with him, but she has that look in her eye. God, this could be really embarrassing.

"Mm hm," says Danny, trying not to talk with his mouth full. "Yes. I've been with the same club since I was little. I'm at the point where I train just about every day."

"Goodness," says Mom, "that's a big time commitment. Is that what you're planning to do when you graduate? I mean, be a professional fighter or something like that?" Oh, she's as subtle as a sledgehammer. As if no one in the room realizes what she's up to. She might as well come out with "How are you planning on providing for my daughter?" and be done with it. But Danny just laughs.

"No," he shakes his head. "I love what I do, but I really want to be a Phys. Ed. teacher. Right now the plan is to go to university, then teacher's college."

Mom's eyebrows go up in pleasant surprise. So do mine—Danny and I have been so concerned about what's going on in the present that we still haven't talked about things like this.

Mom says, "Teaching? Well, that's great. You know, Cass wants to be an archaeologist."

"Really?" replies Danny, looking at me with a smile. "That's really—"

"There!" interrupts Clara, coming back into the room. "Everything's set up so that I can call the social worker first thing in the morning." As she launches back into what tomorrow will bring, Danny leans over and quietly says, "Really cool is what I was going to say. I want to hear more about it. At lunch tomorrow, sound good?"

"Absolutely," I answer. "And you can tell me all about how you want to be a teacher."

Now that Clara's troubles seem to be over, it'll be nice to talk about other things, like the future, for a change.

It's late by the time we get home. Chris has already fallen asleep in the back seat, so I half-carry, half-walk him into the house to give Mom and Grant a minute alone. As much as I have a problem with what Grant represents, I can't help but want Mom to be happy. I'm finding it harder and harder to resent him, especially when he does things like stand up to Mr. Vanelli, or make Mom feel good about herself. In fact, as much as I hate to admit it, he kind of reminds me of my Dad.

I finally manage to get Chris into both his pyjamas and his bed—teeth-brushing is definitely off the table for tonight—when Mom comes upstairs. She laughs softly at the sight of Chris sprawled out across his bed, clutching an Almighty Rat action figure in one fist, and says, "Lord, that child could sleep through a hurricane."

"I know," I reply. "He only opened his eyes long enough to grab the Rat."

We both chuckle, then Mom says, "I know it's late, but I have the kettle on. Feel like a cup of tea?"

"Sure," I answer. "Do we have any peppermint?"

"I think so—I'll go check. Meet you downstairs in a few minutes."

I get my own pyjamas on, wash my face, and then head down. Mom and I have had this tea ritual for years—after Chris is in bed, we sit in the kitchen with our cups of tea and we each talk about our day. Lately we've been letting it slide—what with our fight, and then Clara coming to stay, there wasn't much chance to get together. I'm glad she's suggested it though—I always get a kick out of her work stories. Sometimes they can be really funny, like the guy who wanted to take out life insurance on his pet chinchilla, or the idiot burglar who wanted to sue a family because he fell off their roof trying to break into their house (he claimed they were negligent because they hadn't cleared the snow off the roof properly). And then there were the tragic stories, like the family who lost everything in a fire, or the teenage girl who was killed by a drunk driver—you know, stories that remind you how fragile life can really be. As for me, I usually just talk about school, mundane things that let Mom think I'm normal and doing just fine. I always avoid the topic of Dad, and she never pushes me into talking about him. It's funny how two people who've lost something so important can talk for so long without ever acknowledging the loss they share.

Mom has the tea poured, and I can smell the peppermint as I come into the kitchen. I sit down at the table and she passes me my cup with a smile. I ask the question I always ask to start us off.

"So, how was your day?" We both giggle a little.

"Hmm, let's see..." she says. "I'd have to say 'very exciting'. I got to meet my daughter's first boyfriend, I almost got into a fight with a crazy landlord, and I did a lot of heavy lifting. Overall, not your average day. Danny seems very nice, by the way. Absolutely the knight in shining armour type." She gives me a big grin, and I feel myself going red.

"Yeah," I agree. "He is pretty nice. He's—easy to be around." And I mean it—I've never felt so comfortable with anyone before. Being with Danny is like being with someone I've known all my life; I find it hard to believe that I didn't even really know he existed a little over a week ago.

"I know what you mean. Grant's like that too." She smiles into her teacup, then changes the topic. "Are you getting excited about your big date?" she teases.

"Mom!" I protest. "It's not that big a deal—just a little mortal combat, then some pizza." We both laugh. "I get to meet his parents. I'm kind of nervous about it—I've never 'met' a guy's parents before. I hope they like me."

"Oh, honey, of course they will. You're very likeable—just be yourself." She gets up, yawns, and kisses me on the top of my head. "Time for bed, Cass—see you in the morning." She puts her cup in the sink and walks out of the kitchen.

"Yeah, I'll be right up." I sit for a minute longer, drinking my tea and thinking. Just be myself, huh? I'm still not really sure who that is, although when I'm with Danny, I feel like I'm getting closer to it all the time. I like who I am with him, and that's different for me. Definitely something I could get used to.

Chapter 11

My day in school today is pretty much flying by in a blur. I had trouble sleeping last night—my mind just couldn't seem to shut itself off. It was all a jumble of thoughts about Danny, Mom, Grant, Clara, Chris, school, work, the summer coming up... when the alarm went off this morning, it was even more hellacious than normal. As a result, I feel like I have a head full of cotton, and I'm too tired to concentrate on anything more complex than sitting. My Drama teacher, Mr. Schenk, has other ideas.

"Come on," he yells (he's always yelling—it's as though he thinks the louder he is, the more he'll inspire us—unfortunately, it just annoys us). "Be any animal you'd like! Move around the floor! Make me believe!!" Everyone groans and starts shuffling around, doing very poor imitations of elephants and monkeys. I'm doing my best to be a fish, with my hands together out in front, and half-heartedly making guppy noises. God, just tell me what kind of idiot thinks drama games at 8:30 on a Friday morning is fun? I see out of the corner of my eye that Neville Hewitt, head of the Drama Club, is steadfastly and determinedly "being" a crab—so now my question is answered.

"Cass, you're not trying hard enough!! You can be a better horse than that!!!" Mr Schenk yells at me enthusiastically. Horse? Really? I think I'm a pretty believable fish, considering how tired I am. And just to confirm my thoughts, Greg Lawson, one of the stoners who hangs out in the smoke pit, comes crawling by doing what looks like a cat, and says, "Dude, I thought you were a fish. Guess what I am."

"I'm going to say 'cat'," I answer, looking down at him.

"Right you are," he laughs, then sits down and tries to lick his own leg. "How do cats do this?" he asks wonderingly.

"Fan-TASTIC cat, Greg!!!" yells Mr. Schenk. Greg smiles back broadly, and gives Mr. Schenk a thumbs-up. I go back to being the best fish I can be, and pray for lunchtime to come.

By the time lunch rolls around, all I want to do is go home and crawl back into bed, but I'm meeting Danny in the cafeteria, and that energizes me a little. When I get there, he's sitting with Miles. They're both surrounded by food containers and talking enthusiastically about something. I sit down and smile.

"I feel like I'm at a training camp for an eating contest," I say.

Miles laughs. "Gotta keep the energy up, you know."

"Yep," Danny agrees. "My weigh-in last night was fine, so now it's time to start packing in the proteins, carbs, and sugars. Best part about tournaments."

"Yeah, I can see how much you're enjoying yourself," I reply. We all laugh and Miles says, "Well, I'm done for now. Carry on eating, Dan-o. There's a pack of Twinkies over there that you seem to have missed."

Danny grabs for the package as Miles gets up. "Thanks, man. See you later."

He turns his attention to me. "So I had a really fun time last night—your family is great. How long has your Mom been with Grant? He seems like a good guy."

"Yeah, I guess so," I admit grudgingly. "I'm actually not sure how long they've been dating—it's been kind of weird." I give him the short version of how I found out about Grant, and he puts his hand over mine with a look of concern.

"Wow, that must have been really hard for you—it sounds like you've given up a lot for your mom and Chris. I don't blame you for being angry."

"Yeah, well, I'm over it now, pretty well. Mom and I are fine. I just can't figure out why she didn't tell me for so long. It made it worse that she didn't trust me."

"Maybe it wasn't that she didn't trust you—maybe she was worried that it would seem like she was trying to replace your Dad and she didn't want to hurt you," he says. "I think she loves you a lot."

This is all starting to get too close for comfort. I know he's right, and I know he cares, but I'm not ready to start delving into my feelings about Dad, especially when I'm so tired, so I say, "I know. But listen, you were going to tell me about your plans for teaching."

He instinctively seems to understand that I need to talk about something else, and he switches gears just as fast. "Right—and you were going to tell me about wanting to be an archaeologist." We spend the rest of lunch focused on the future. I don't tell him about how the archaeology thing started out as a joke, because honestly, I don't feel like it's a joke anymore—I'm actually giving it serious consideration, and having to pass up the camp this summer is bothering me more and more.

◆ ◆ ◆

You Jane store is a madhouse when I get there. We're having our semi-annual clearance sale, trying to get rid of the last of the winter styles, so I don't get a chance to talk to Clara until break. Since she's the assistant manager now, she's kind of my boss, which is different, but she's made up a really fair schedule for the next two weeks, and she made sure everyone was getting their break on time, so I'm not too worried about it. When it's time for my break, she steps out for a minute with me. We go to the food court to grab a couple of burgers from Happy Burger Time. While we're waiting in line, she blurts out, "I get Lindsay back tomorrow!"

"That's fantastic, Clara—when did you find out?"

"This afternoon. The social worker came by to see the apartment, my work schedule and everything, and said I could pick her up from the foster home she's in tomorrow afternoon. I talked to Lindsay a little while ago and she's really excited. She said the foster family has been pretty nice, but she can't wait to see the apartment and the new school she'll be going to."

"That's great. So how is your new place?" I ask.

"It's coming along. I haven't had a lot of time to unpack yet, what with my new work schedule," she smiles.

"Yeah, I noticed," I reply. "You're working days from now on."

"Well, it's the best thing for Lindsay. She's too young to be at home by herself, so I have to work while she's in school. Then I can be there for her at night and on weekends. It's just making it hard to get anything else done right now, and I really wanted her room to be completely set up and decorated by the time she got home. I found this really awesome princess-style headboard this morning at the second-hand store—you should have seen the looks I got trying to wrestle it onto the bus—but I'm not sure how to attach it to the bed."

"Why don't I come over tomorrow and give you a hand?" I offer. "I can bring some screwdrivers and wrenches — I'm sure we can figure it out together. Then we can finish decorating."

"Really?!" she exclaims. "That would be amazing. You're such a good friend — I don't deserve you."

"Don't be ridiculous," I answer. "I live to assemble furniture. It's my favourite thing to do. Besides, Mom and Grant are taking Chris to the movies, so I really have nothing else going on. You're actually doing me the favour."

We both laugh, and she says, "Anything to help you out, Cass. Come over whenever you feel like it."

"No problem — I can be there by ten. We'll be able to get everything done before you pick up Lindsay."

Clara is happy, but she doesn't realize that I wasn't kidding when I said she was doing me a favour. I've never really had much chance to just hang out and do things with a friend, so this is as much for me as for her, and I'm looking forward to it.

Chapter 12

Well, it looks like any hope I still had for archaeology camp is gone now. It's my own fault, I guess. I was at Clara's and we were having a lot of fun. We finally got the bed put together after a couple of tries — the first time the frame wasn't secure enough and the whole thing collapsed when Clara lay on it, and the second time, we accidentally put the headboard on backwards, and had to take it off and start again. Finally, though, the unpacking was done, the wallpaper border was up, and everything looked great. We took a break and Clara made us a late lunch of bologna sandwiches and orange pop — her culinary skills need a little work — and we sat, admiring our handiwork. Then Clara said, "Everything is working out so well. I just have one more problem that I have to deal with."

"What is it?" I asked.

"Well, I realized last night after I got home that I hadn't thought about the summer. Lindsay's too young to stay by herself when I'm working — I'm not taking a chance with that because if the social worker found out, I could lose guardianship — and I have to work at least 40 hours a week to make enough money to keep the apartment. I can't afford to send her to camps or anything like that, but I could afford to pay a babysitter to look after her. So I was thinking..." She paused.

"Thinking what?" I asked. Honestly, at this point I had no idea what she was getting at.

"Well... you take care of your little brother in the summer, right? So I was wondering if maybe, if I paid you, you could look after Lindsay as well. You can say no; I would totally understand." She looked at me with a pleading expression. I didn't know what to say. How could I explain that I was secretly hoping in my heart that somehow everything would work out and I could take the job at that camp up north when I knew in my head that there was no way it would ever happen? What kind of excuse could I even think up? She was sitting and staring at me, holding her breath, like I was her only chance for true happiness.

"Oh," I said, "that shouldn't be a problem." And there went any chance of me finally getting to do something I wanted. Clara let out a huge sigh of relief and said, "Thank you so much. After what she's been through, I hated the thought of her being with a total stranger all summer. She'll have so much fun with you and Chris — there's the park and the zoo and swimming and..." She kept going in an excited rush about all the things I could do with the kids, and I just sat and smiled.

I'm still feeling pretty down about having to give up on my summer dreams, but that all starts to fade as it gets closer to the time when Danny and his parents are supposed to pick me up. I go down to the kitchen, where Mom is making a breakfast of pancakes, bacon, and eggs, and sit down at the table. She looks at me out of the corner of her eye and asks, "Hungry?"

"Not really," I answer. In truth, I'm starting to get really nervous. Since Danny is in the tournament, I'll be spending a lot of the day with just his parents. I'm not great with people I don't know as it is—will they expect me to talk a lot, or be really bubbly or something? And if I'm not, will Danny be disappointed? Even though what Mom's cooking smells amazing, I think if I eat anything, I might throw up.

As if she can read my mind, Mom comes over and hugs me. "Cass, you're going to be fine. They'll love you, I know they will. And you look beautiful, so don't worry."

"Thanks, Mom" I sigh. "So what movie are you guys going to see?"

Mom laughs. "The latest adventures of the Almighty Rat—what else?!"

"I know," I answer with a smile. "You've got to love his loyalty to that crazy Asian rodent. Have fun. And don't worry about the dishes—I'll clean them up before I leave."

When the house is finally quiet, and I've finished the dishes, I have nothing else to do except pace the floor, waiting for Danny and his parents to arrive. When they do arrive, a little early, it's in a big SUV, the back filled to almost-overflowing with athletic bags, water bottles, and an assortment of sports equipment. I watch from the window as Danny comes jogging up to the front door. He's a bundle of barely contained energy, and I open the door before he has a chance to knock.

"Hey!" he says in happy surprise.

"Hey yourself," I answer back. We just look at each other, smiling, then he asks, "Are you ready to go? I know we're early, but I wanted to get in a good warm-up before my fight."

"Yeah, no, it's great, let's go," I stammer. He looks at me quizzically and takes my hand as we walk towards the SUV. "Are you nervous about meeting my parents?" he teases.

"No, of course not!" I say defiantly. "I'm sure they're very nice people."

"Yeah, they are." He grins at me and tugs my hand. "Come on."

His dad is a good-looking, well-built man with an easy-going smile, and his mom is petite and blonde, with green eyes just like Danny's. They greet me warmly as I climb into the back seat, and my nerves start to melt away a little. On the way to the college where the tournament is being held, they keep the conversation moving, asking me questions about school and my family, teasing Danny, and each other. I get the sense that they have a solid family relationship, and that there's no tension between them.

"Have you ever been to a kickboxing tournament before, Cass?" his dad asks.

"No, it's my first time. I'm not quite sure what to expect," I answer.

"Oh, it's great fun —," his dad starts to answer, but he's cut off by Danny's mom, who continues, " — if you don't mind seeing your only child get hit in the face!"

"Ah, mom," Danny protests, "you know that hardly ever happens. And I'm wearing a helmet and mouthguard." She mock-pouts and they all laugh.

"Is that all the equipment you're allowed to wear?" I ask. I have no clue what kickboxers wear — if it was me, I'd want full body armour.

"Yeah, that and shin guards and gloves," he answers.

"And a cup," his mom chimes in. "Don't forget about that!"

Danny looks absolutely mortified and stares straight ahead, not saying anything. I can't help but snicker, and his dad gives his mom a poke.

"What?!" she exclaims innocently, looking around at us. "Shouldn't I have said that in front of your girl-friend?"

Danny inhales sharply, and looks even more painfully embarrassed. I feel so sorry for him that I just pat his hand and say, "Good, I'm glad you're 'well-protected'," with an emphasis on the word 'protected', just to tease him a little. He laughs softly and relaxes.

When we arrive at the college, Danny's parents get out and start unloading the SUV. Danny turns to me and says hesitantly, "You're not mad, are you?"

I look at him in bewilderment. "Mad about what?"

"You know—the whole 'girlfriend' thing. My mom gets a little ahead of herself sometimes. I wouldn't want you to think—"

"No," I quickly reassure him. "It's not a problem, I'm not mad at all. It was—sweet."

Actually, I'm just fine with it. I've never been somebody's girlfriend before, and if Danny's family thinks of me that way, then great. I just wonder if HE does. As if he can read my thoughts, he says tentatively, "Because, I kind of think of you in my head as my girlfriend. You know, because you're a girl and you're my friend..."

"So I'm your girlfriend. And since you're a boy and you're my friend, I guess that makes you..."

I wait for him to answer, which he does with a big smile, "Your boyfriend. I'm glad that's all settled then."

We get the rest of the equipment and bags and go inside. I'm walking on air, thinking, 'Yep, my boyfriend is going to kick some ass', followed by 'God, I hope my boyfriend doesn't get his nose broken'. Either way, apparently he's my boyfriend.

It's crowded inside the gym where they have the ring set up. Danny's fight is later in the schedule, after a couple of exhibition matches, the women's division, and junior kickboxing. He tells us to find seats in the stands while he goes to meet with his trainer and warm up. Easier said than done, until I spot Miles waving madly at us. We climb into the stands and sit down next to him.

"I saved you seats," he says to me. "Hi, Mr. and Mrs. Stryker."

"Hey, Miles, it's good to see you. Thanks for the seats!" Danny's dad answers. "How's the wrestling going?" He and Miles start talking about his latest competition as the first of the exhibition matches starts. The announcer, a tough-looking old guy, explains that the exhibition matches are first fights for new kickboxers, so they're just trying to get some experience and not actually hurt each other. That sounds very ominous to me—does that mean in the other matches, they will be trying to hurt each other? Even still, the punches and kicks these 'new fighters' are laying on each other look pretty intense to me. Then the women's division starts. I've never seen women, well, teenage girls really, hammering away at each other with such serious intent to inflict pain. Then the first match ends, and the two girls take off their helmets and gloves and hug each other like they're old friends. And I guess they are, because Miles leans over and says, "That was a great fight! Martine and Trang train together at the same club as Danny. It was hard to tell who was going to win for a while there, they're both so good."

"How do you know who won? I can't tell!" I say. "It looks really complicated."

Miles is busy trying to explain the complex scoring system to me when suddenly I see Danny coming out towards the ring. He looks amazing—he's wearing silk boxing shorts and his equipment, but I hadn't realized until this moment how muscular he is.

"Danny's proud of his six-pack," laughs Miles.

"Mm-hmm," I answer. I can't think of anything else to say to that.

Then I spot Danny's opponent. He's not much bigger than Danny, since they're in the same weight class, but he seems really solid. His nose looks like it's been broken more than once, and he has a huge skull tattoo across his back.

"That's Miro," says Miles. "He's pretty good, but Danny's beaten him before."

The first round starts—Miles explains that there are three rounds of two minutes each—and there's a lot of initial circling and sizing up the opponent. They seem as though they're testing each other, feeling out each other's weak spots. The first round ends without much contact, which is fine by me, and by Danny's mom as well, if the way she's twisting the straps of her purse is any indication. At the bell to start the second round, Danny moves in, looking confident and aggressive. He never takes his eyes off Miro. He's completely focused and seems ready to strike at any minute. Suddenly, like a flash, Danny moves in and throws a hard punch. Miro deflects it, counters with a kick, and the fight really begins. By the time the second round is over, they're both panting and covered in sweat as they retreat to their corners to talk strategy with their trainers.

Danny's trainer isn't what I expected. I thought he'd be big and mean-looking, kind of like an older version of Miles, but he's actually an elderly man wearing khakis and loafers. I say to Miles, "Are you sure Danny's trainer knows what to tell him?"

Miles chuckles. "Danny's trainer is Jake Larson—haven't you heard of him? In his day, he was a nationally ranked boxer—he actually went to the Olympics, then he turned pro. He started a combined boxing/kickboxing/martial arts club 30 years ago. Trust me, I wouldn't want to go head to head with him. He may look old, but he's still fast—and strong!"

Jake is leaning over Danny, whispering to him with ferocious intensity, while Danny is nodding vigorously. I can see now that Miles wasn't kidding—whatever he's telling Danny, it's pumping him up for the next round. When the buzzer goes, Danny hits the ring like a tornado in a flurry of punches and kicks. It's all Miro can do to stay upright for the first minute, Danny has him so off-balance. Then suddenly, he refocuses and comes up under Danny's guard just long enough to hit him hard in the face. Danny is stunned for a second and the crowd gasps. Mrs. Stryker twists her purse straps, her knuckles white, and winces as though she can feel the punch too. The ref steps up with a questioning look, but Danny waves him off, gives his head a shake, and is right back in there. By the time the final buzzer sounds, Miro's taken a couple of hard punches as well, one that made him stagger against the ropes, and they both look exhausted. As they wait for the judges' decision, I ask Miles, "Who won?"

Miles answers, "It was pretty even until Danny came out so hard in the last round. I've got to give it to him, but we'll see what the judges say."

The judges call the referee over and say something to him, then he goes back to the middle of the ring where Danny and Miro are waiting. He takes both their hands, and without hesitation, hoists Danny's arm high in the air. The crowd starts cheering wildly, and Danny's parents hug each other. Danny and Miro take off their gloves, shake hands, then pat each other on the back. The referee puts a medal around Danny's neck and the crowd goes crazy again. As Danny leaves the ring, Jake is there, and they high-five each other and laugh. Jake looks at Danny's eye, which is really swollen from Miro's punch, and says something serious to Danny, who smiles and nods, then they go to the change room together. The rest of the fights aren't anywhere near as exciting, so I'm happy that Danny doesn't take long. When he comes out into the stands, freshly showered and changed into regular clothes, people are high-fiving him and slapping him on the back as he makes his way up to us. He squeezes in between me and his mom, who takes one look at his eye and says, "Oh, Danny!"

"Don't worry, Mom—it's not as bad as it looks," he reassures her.

"Awesome fight, man!" exclaims Miles. He and Danny start going over it in detail. I don't understand a lot of the terminology, but I listen with fascination, thinking, 'My boyfriend was the winner', and enjoying the way it sounds.

Chapter 13

When the tournament is over, Danny's parents drop us off at Fabrizio's, the local pizza place, and tell us to call them when we want to be picked back up. We find a quiet table in a dimly-lit corner where Danny's swollen eye won't be quite so noticeable, although it doesn't seem to be bothering him at all. In fact, I'd swear he's proud of it, the way he keeps grinning at me. The waiter comes over, and it's obvious that he's trying not to stare at Danny's eye, and that he's dying to ask what happened, but he's too polite. We order salads, and I ask for a small Hawaiian, while Danny goes for the large meat-lovers. I snicker, and he says, "What? I'm hungry!"

"I know. You deserve it after the way you fought today. It was really cool to watch, although I had my hands over my eyes half the time! I don't know how your mom stands it—she was clenching her fists and her teeth for all three rounds."

"I know—it's hard for me too, knowing that she's so worried, but I just have to concentrate on not getting hit as much as I hit the other guy. Luckily, it worked out that way today."

We talk for a while longer about the fight, the scoring, and admire Danny's medal. The salad and pizzas arrive, and Danny launches into his with gusto. I just pick away at mine; I'm starting to feel a little down again about everything. Danny must have noticed, because he suddenly swallows, looks at me and says, "Hey, what's the matter? Isn't the pizza good?"

"No, no, the pizza's fine," I reassure him. "Nothing's wrong."

"Are you sure?" he asks. "All of a sudden you just seem kind of sad."

I'm about to tell him I'm OK again, but he looks at me with so much concern that, before I even realize it, I'm spilling my guts to him about the archaeology camp, my responsibilities to Chris and Mom, offering to take care of Lindsay, and how miserable I am about all of it. When I'm done, he leans back in his chair, and says, "This is an easy one to fix."

"What do you mean?" I ask incredulously. "It can't be fixed — it's just the way it is, and I have to live with it."

"No, you don't," he answers. "That punch in the face must have knocked some sense into me, because I have the perfect solution already."

I look at him warily. "What solution?"

"Simple," he says. "You take the job up north, and I look after Chris and Lindsay while you're gone."

I stare at him in shock. "But you don't want to do that. And besides, my mom can't afford to pay a babysitter — that's why I'm doing it!"

He laughs. "Well, first, I do want to do it. If I'm going to be a teacher, I'll need experience working with kids, right? I can put on my resume that I ran a mini-daycare or something. Second, I don't need any money — Clara doesn't have to pay me either. I work with my Dad whenever I feel like it, and he pays me more than enough. Besides, I like Chris and Lindsay — we'll have fun together. Then when you're back, you can take over, and I can spend the rest of the summer working with my Dad."

I sit back hard in my chair, in disbelief. Is he really willing to do this for me? It seems too good to be true. As much as I want to, I know I can't let him. "No," I say firmly. "I appreciate the offer, but it's not fair to you to spend all of July with two little kids and not get paid for it."

"Oh, come on, Cass — you know it's the best solution. At least think about it."

I groan and put my head in my hands. "OK, I'll think about it," I promise. It's so tempting — taking off for a month without worrying about Chris or finances, getting to do something for me for a change, making extra money to put away for school — no, I can't let myself get carried away like this. Still, it was so thoughtful that he offered that I find myself perking up and digging into the pizza, much to Danny's amusement.

When we're finished eating, and Danny has insisted on paying for the whole dinner, we call his parents and wait outside the restaurant for them. As we're standing there talking, I see, out of the corner of my eye, Megan Pearson, that nasty little gossip girl, across the street. Sure enough, she spies us, and immediately pulls out her cell phone and starts texting as she scurries down the street. Well, who cares what she says or who she says it to? Here's what I predict: she'll end up married to some jock named Billy who gets a beer belly by the age of 30, and sits in his lounge chair watching football and drinking with 'the boys' all weekend, while she slugs wine coolers on the patio with curlers in her hair and a trashy romance novel in her hand, wondering how it got to be like this and fantasizing that she's still back in high school. It would serve her right. But everyone knows that the best revenge is a life lived well, and right now, things are going pretty well, so she can text all she wants about me and Danny together at Fabrizio's.

He sees me looking down the street with a frown and gives me a curious glance. I smile back and take his hand until his parents arrive.

When we get to my house, Danny gets out of the car too, and walks me to the door.

"I had a fantastic time," I tell him. "The kickboxing, dinner, your parents, everything was great."

"Me too," he agrees. We stare at each other for a minute, then I say, "Well, I guess I better get in..."

"Right," he says, then takes a deep breath and steps towards me. He puts his hand on my shoulder, then leans in and kisses me on the lips. We kind of linger like that for a minute, my knees getting weaker by the second, then the porch light comes on and he steps back. "Well, good night then," he says. "I'll see you at school tomorrow."

I'm breathless, but I manage to get out "Yeah, see you tomorrow." He walks back towards the car, but turns half-way to give me a smile and a wave. I wave back, still a little stunned. I realize that I better try to wipe the goofy grin off my face before I go in the house, or everyone will know I just had my first real kiss, but I don't know if it's possible.

When I get in the house, Mom is sitting on the couch with the TV turned down low. She's trying to play it cool, but I can tell she's just dying to know how my big date went.

"Hi, Mom," I say nonchalantly.

"Hey, honey," she replies. She can barely keep the smile off her face. "Did you have a good time?"

"Yeah, it was a lot of fun." I leave it at that, just to see how long it will be before she can't take it anymore. I sit down at the opposite end of the couch and smile at her. She's literally squirming with excitement, but trying to cover it up. I love it.

"So," she says. "When I heard the car pull up, I put the kettle on. The tea's brewing if you want some." This is her invitation to sit and share details.

"Sure. Sounds good," I answer, and she jumps up to get the tea. She's back in record time with two cups, which she puts down on the coffee table to cool.

"Oh, by the way," she says. "Clara called while you were out. She's invited us to a house-warming dinner tomorrow night. I can't go, but I thought you and Chris might be able to."

"Sure, thanks. I'll text her later and let her know." We sit in silence. She looks like she's about to jump out of her skin.

"So?" she says again, staring me down.

"So? What?" I answer. I'm starting to enjoy myself—I don't get to tease her very much—but then she wails, "Oh, come on, Cass, be fair! Aren't you going to tell me about it?!"

I laugh. "Of course I am—I was just having a little fun with you, that's all."

She says, "Very funny," and gives me a light slap on the arm. "Now, spill the beans."

I do, giving her a blow-by-blow description of the car ride, what his parents are like, the fight, dinner (leaving out Danny's offer), and when I get to the part where we're on the front porch, she looks at me with expectation. I really don't want to get into the details of the kiss, especially not with my mother, so I just say, "That's it."

She looks disappointed. "Didn't he—kiss you?" she whispers.

"Mother! Nice girls don't kiss and tell. And now, goodnight—I have school in the morning." I take my cup and start to go upstairs. From behind me, she calls out, "Ha! If you're not telling, then he must have kissed you. Hehe!" She giggles and kicks her feet up. I laugh quietly to myself—I think she's as excited as I am about the whole thing. I get ready for bed, give Clara a quick text telling her to expect Chris and me at five, then I try to go to sleep. It's going to be another one of those mind-racing nights—I can tell.

Chapter 14

Sure enough, I spend the day in a groggy fog, thanks to the minimal amount of sleep I got the night before. Believe it or not, it wasn't the kiss I was thinking about—it was Danny's offer that I couldn't get out of my mind. I went back and forth with it, weighing the pros and cons. There were so many pros, but the biggest con was that I felt like I would be abandoning Chris. I couldn't do that to him—he was my responsibility. I finally made up my mind around three in the morning that I would turn down Danny's offer to look after Chris and Lindsay while I went up north. There was always next summer—maybe Mr. Pratt's friend in the archaeology department would hire me then. When I see Danny at lunch, he doesn't mention it again, and neither do I. His eye is looking less swollen, but the purple had turned into a rainbow of colour. He gets some looks as we walk down the hall together at the end of the day, and there's a lot of whispering, no doubt thanks to Megan Pearson, but we both just ignore it.

I start packing up my books, and say to him, "Clara's invited Chris and me over for dinner tonight. Why don't you come too? I'm sure she won't mind."

"I'd love to," he says, "but I have kung fu and conditioning class tonight. Can't miss that. Plus, my trainer is giving me a 'debrief' about my fight yesterday. He recorded it so that we could watch it back and see where my weaknesses were..." He keeps talking but I'm not listening anymore, because at this moment, Tommy Fillmore walks by. He doesn't say anything out loud, because Danny's standing right there, but he mouths the word 'slut' at me, and makes a rude hand gesture. As I watch him walk down the hall, I realize that Danny has stopped talking and is staring after him too.

"Is that jerk still bothering you?" he asks.

"No, it's fine," I answer. I'm furious, but I don't want Danny getting himself in trouble. I vow to myself that the next time Tommy says something to me, I'm going to tell him off.

Chris and I get to Clara's apartment just before five o'clock. Chris is really excited—he hardly ever gets to ride the bus, so this is a double treat for him. Clara's apartment looks great now that she's finished decorating and unpacking, and whatever she's cooking for dinner smells pretty good too. It doesn't take more than a minute after we introduce Chris and Lindsay to each other that they've gone off to Lindsay's room to play a board game that the foster family gave her as a goodbye present.

"They were pretty decent people," Clara says. "It could have been a lot worse, but I'm so happy I've got her here with me now."

"She looks pretty happy too," I reply. "I'll bet she loved her new room."

"Yep, she loved it all right. She never had anything like that when we were living with Mom," she says bitterly. "All Mom cared about was her boyfriends and her beer—we could have slept on the floor for all that it mattered to her." Then she perks up and says, "Well, that's over with now. I don't think any court in the world would take Lindsay away from me and give her back to Mom, even if she wanted her, which I doubt."

"There's no chance your Dad will come back and ask for custody, is there?"

"That jerk? Not a chance," Clara replies angrily, then says more quietly, "But Lindsay isn't his anyway. Even Mom isn't sure who her father is. Pretty sad, huh? So, are you hungry?"

I nod. "Yeah, what are you cooking? It smells great!"

"Don't laugh," she says. "I found this recipe in a magazine for tuna casserole. God, I feel like such a grown-up. Tuna casserole, assistant manager, legal guardian—me—can you believe it?"

"Yes," I laugh. "Everybody has to grow up some-time, right? Anyway, Chris and I both love tuna casserole, so don't worry, old lady."

When we finally sit down to eat, I realize that Clara has gone to a lot of trouble. In addition to the casserole, there's salad, fresh rolls, steamed broccoli, cooked carrots, and an assortment of cheeses.

"Wow, Clara," I say. "You didn't have to go to so much trouble. This looks amazing!"

"It's the least I could do after all the help you've given me. I wish your mom could have come too."

The food tastes great, and we're half-way through the meal, when suddenly we hear some kind of commotion coming from the hallway. Someone is yelling, and it's get-ting closer by the second.

"What on earth is that?" Clara exclaims, jumping up from the table and going to the door.

She looks through the peephole as the noise be-comes louder and more clear. Someone is yelling, "Clara!" at the top of his lungs.

"Oh my God!" Clara gasps. "It's Frank! What the hell is he doing here?! Cass, get the kids into Lindsay's bedroom!" I hustle Chris and Lindsay into her room; they both look terrified.

"Just stay in here, OK guys? Don't worry, everything's going to be fine." I run back to the door. Frank has started hammering on it, and Clara is in a panic.

"Clara, we have to call the police!" I cry out over the pounding. Frank has started yelling, "Clara, I know you're in there! Let me in!"

"We can't!" she wails. "If the police show up, who knows what the landlord will think, and if I lose this place, I'll lose guardianship of Lindsay!"

The pounding and yelling continues, and now we can hear the sounds of other voices and other doors slamming. Clara runs to the door and says, "The chain's on—I'll just open it a crack and try to calm him down, then maybe he'll go away!"

"No, Clara, don't—!" I call out, as she starts to open the door. The second she does, Frank slams his whole weight into it. With a sickening crack, the chain breaks and the door flies open. Frank stands there, panting. He reeks of alcohol.

"There you are, you little bitch," he says in a low voice. "I've been looking for you. Nice of you to leave a forwarding address with that slime bag Vanelli."

"What do you want, Frank?" Clara asks, her voice shaking.

"I get kicked out of my house, thrown in jail, and lose my job, all because of you, and you want to know what I want?!" His voice is getting louder and more ominous by the second, and he starts to advance towards her.

"Look—," I begin, trying to intervene.

Then everything starts to happen so fast it's still all a blur. Frank comes at me and pushes me back, then suddenly Chris comes flying out of the bedroom, hollering "Leave my sister alone!" He tries to karate chop Frank, who bats him aside hard, launching him into the air. He hits the wall headfirst and crumples to the ground in a heap, unconscious. I scream and run to Chris, Clara grabs a knife off the table and starts shouting at Frank to get out, neighbours are calling out "Phone the police!" and "We already did!", and Lindsay is sitting in the doorway to her bedroom crying. It's absolute pandemonium when we hear the first of the sirens. The police pull up in front of the building just as Frank takes off, right into the arms of a waiting officer, who promptly throws him to the ground and cuffs him. More cops are pounding up the stairs, as I'm crying for someone to call an ambulance, and trying to wake Chris up. Suddenly there are paramedics with a stretcher; they tell me to step back, then they pick Chris up, put him on it, and check his vital signs. I'll do anything to have him be OK, anything. What will I do if he dies?! How will I ever forgive myself? It's too much, and I fall to the floor, weeping.

One of the paramedics comes over and says quietly, "Hey, is that your brother?" I nod and keep crying. He says, "He's taken a pretty hard knock to the head, but he's going to be alright. See?"

I look up and realize that Chris has his eyes open and he's talking to the paramedic, who's asking him questions and holding up his fingers. I run over to the stretcher, and Chris says sleepily, "Hi Cass. What happened?"

"You tried to beat up Frank, you goof," I smile through my tears, stroking his hair. "Not a great idea."

"If I'd been wearing my Almighty Rat suit, I would've kicked his butt," he answers, then closes his eyes again.

The paramedic closest to Chris starts saying, "Come on, Chris, open your eyes, open your eyes." I turn to the paramedic with a look of fear, but he says, "Don't worry—it's a concussion—a big one, but he's going to be OK. He'll need a little time to recover, but the most important thing right now is that we keep him conscious. We're going to take him to the hospital and he'll have to stay overnight.

You should probably call your parents so they can meet us there."

Chris has his eyes open again, and the paramedics are talking to him, and getting him to answer more questions, like "what's your middle name?" and "what year were you born?", so I call Mom on my cell phone and brace myself for her reaction.

Understandably, she's really upset, but she tells me it's not my fault, and not to blame myself. We agree that I'll ride in the ambulance with Chris, and she'll meet us at the hospital. When I get off the phone, Clara comes over. She's all teary and says, "I'm so sorry, Cass. I thought if I just talked to him..."

"It's OK, Clara. Don't worry about it. They say Chris will be just fine. You couldn't have known that Frank would do any of that."

"God, I should never have told Vanelli where I was moving to. Trust him to tell a psycho like Frank where I live!" She starts to cry in earnest, and Lindsay runs over to her. They hug each other, and Clara says, "What a great start to my grown-up life." I join the hug.

Chris calls out from the stretcher, "Hey! Why is everybody crying? That guy's gone now!" We all look at him and laugh. I have to work hard to convince Clara that she and Lindsay don't have to come to the hospital with us; besides the police need to talk to them about what happened. The officer in charge tells me that I can go, that someone will take my statement once we get to County General, so we load Chris up and head off.

Mom is already there when we arrive, looking sick and worried. She runs to Chris as he's being wheeled in, and smothers him with kisses, much to his horror, while he's being admitted.

"Mom, I'm fine!" he protests, and it certainly seems from the way he's struggling to get away from her smooches that he's telling the truth. Once he's put into a room, the doctor comes in to check him over. A police officer is waiting in the hall to take my statement, so I leave Mom with Chris and the doctor and step out.

I tell the officer, Sergeant Tanaka, everything that happened, making sure that I get all the details right; I don't want to take a chance that Frank will get away with what he did to Chris.

The sergeant thanks me and says, "We've been looking for this guy for a long time on several outstanding warrants for all kinds of nasty things. Not someone I'd want around my kids, that's for sure. I hope your brother's feeling up to talking to me—if not, I can come back tomorrow."

I check with Mom, and Chris perks up. "I want to talk to the police!" he says. "I feel fine, you know." The doctor agrees that Chris is well enough, and Mom stays with him while he gives his statement. I take a minute to text Danny and let him know what's going on. He calls me back almost right away, and I explain what happened in more detail. He's as relieved as I am that Chris is going to be OK.

"Do you want me to come to the hospital? I can be there in 20 minutes," he offers.

"No, that's OK. Visiting hours are almost over, and Mom's going to drive me home as soon as Chris is done talking to the police. Then she's coming back here to stay the night with him."

"Well, if you're sure," he says. "Then I'll meet you at your locker before class starts, all right? God, I wish I'd been there!"

As much as I'm happy that he cares so much, I'm equally happy that he wasn't there. I know Danny is strong and quick—after seeing him in action the other day, I have no doubt that he could take on almost anybody—but Frank was drunk or stoned, or maybe both, and totally out of control. Who knows what might have happened?

In the car on the way home, I don't say anything and neither does Mom. I don't blame her if she IS angry with me. I was supposed to be taking care of Chris, so it's really my fault that he got hurt. I should have—well, I don't know what I should have done, but I can't shake this feeling of overwhelming guilt.

I start to get teary again, and Mom says again, "Cass, listen to me—it's not your fault. There's no way you could have known that any of this would happen. And there was nothing you could do about it. Once Chris is better, he and I are going to have a very serious conversation about the fact that he is not the Almighty Rat, and doesn't have superpowers. It's one thing being brave and another being reckless."

"Don't be too hard on him, Mom. Seriously, if he hadn't come to my rescue, I don't know what Frank would have done to us. He was really brave—reckless, as well, yes—but I think he's been punished enough."

Mom relents a little and says, "Fine, I won't be hard on him. But we're still going to have a talk about cartoons and reality."

She drops me off, and I go up to my room. I look in the mirror—my face is a mess, all puffy and red. Hopefully, a good night's sleep will do me some good. I'm so tired that I don't even bother to change. I just fall onto the bed, and the next thing I know, it's morning.

Chapter 15

Despite my exhaustion, I wake up early, hoping that Mom will call soon. Sure enough, I'm not out of bed five minutes when the phone rings.

"Good news," Mom tells me. "Chris is fine, and the doctor says I can bring him home in a couple of hours."

"Fantastic—what a relief," I say. "I'm just going to school to get some books that I need, then I'll come home and look after him so you can go to work."

"Will you really? That's so thoughtful of you, honey. I'll see you when you get back."

"Oh, but can you call the office and let them know that I'll be off today?" I ask, and give her the number.

If I'm being perfectly honest, the trip to school for books is an excuse; I just really want to see Danny. I eat a quick breakfast, then rush out the door. Then I decide that rushing isn't a very good idea. I'm shaky and a bit disoriented from being so tired and stressed out. Everything seems a little too bright, and my head is starting to pound in time with my heartbeat. All I really want to do is talk to Danny, then go back home to be with Chris.

I get to my locker—no sign of Danny yet, but I'm early. The halls are crowded and the noise is almost unbearable, considering the way I feel right now. I'm just putting the books I need in my backpack, when Tommy Filmore walks by, and slam! He purposely bumps into me, knocking me into my locker, then calls me a name which I can't even repeat. I'm so furious, that before I even realize it, I've thrown my backpack at him. It hits him hard, and he turns around, then sneers at me.

"You bitch! What was that for?" he asks angrily.

"Are you kidding me?" I yell. "What do you think it was for, you jerk?! Do you think I like being called disgusting names by a sleazebag like you?!"

People are stopping to stare, wondering what all the commotion is. Tommy looks uncomfortable, gives me a dismissive wave of his hand, and turns to walk away.

"Where are you going, big man? Off to harass another girl who won't go out with you? You're pathetic, you know that?! A pathetic excuse for a human being! And don't ever push me or hit me again!!" People are murmuring and pointing, but I'm beside myself with fury at this point—I know I'm provoking Tommy, but I've had more than enough of him. He turns and his face is red with rage and embarrassment.

"What did you say to me?!" He starts advancing toward me, menacingly. I hold my ground as he gets nearer, but I'm starting to panic inside. Would he really attack me in front of this crowd? I start looking around for something to protect myself with, to throw at him if he gets too close, but my books are all in my backpack, which is inconveniently down the hall where it landed.

"What did you say to me?!!" he demands again, this time louder.

Suddenly I hear a voice cut through the crowded hall. "She said you were a pathetic excuse for a human being. Are you deaf as well, asshole?" Then I realize it's

Danny, pushing his way towards me, Miles close behind. Tommy looks startled and turns, then his eyes narrow.

"Stryker, I might have known you'd show up to protect your girlfriend." He spits out the word 'girlfriend' like it leaves a bad taste in his mouth. "And you've brought back-up with you as well. What's the matter — afraid to take me on all by yourself?"

Miles laughs, then steps back and says to Tommy, "He's all yours if you want him." Tommy starts to advance on Danny, who stands his ground.

"Tommy, you know this won't end well for you," Danny says seriously. "Just walk away before you get hurt."

Tommy launches himself at Danny, fists swinging. Danny just sidesteps him, and as Tommy goes by, Danny grabs his arm, twists it behind Tommy's back, and pushes him to the ground.

"Come on, Tommy, you don't want to do this," he says, as Tommy is struggling to get back to his feet. The crowd around us is starting to get more rowdy, and someone begins chanting, "Fight, fight." Other people join in, which draws more students into the hallway.

Tommy manages to regain his footing — he looks enraged, while Danny just stands there staring at him coolly. He runs forward and throws a punch at Danny, who blocks it, and then, in a move that leaves the crowd gasping in amazement, he spins around low and sweeps Tommy's feet out from under him.

Tommy lands on the floor with a thud, and Danny says, "Give it up, man. I could do this all day." The crowd ripples with laughter, and even I snicker a little, mainly because I know that even if Tommy does manage to get up again, he'll only be back on the floor in a manner of seconds — he's way too slow for Danny, and everyone else realizes it too.

Tommy makes a half-hearted effort to get back up. Danny sighs and takes his hands out of his hoodie pockets, ready to take Tommy down again, when the crowd begins to part at the back. I hear adult voices calling out, "Move aside!", "Everyone get to class!", and "What's going on here?!" It's our two vice-principals, Ms. Johnson and Mr. Verde, and they look very unhappy. The students start to disperse, not wanting to be involved in the aftermath of a good fight, and quickly, it's just Danny, Tommy, and me. Tommy is still bent over, shaking his head and breathing hard; Danny comes over to me and puts a protective arm around my shoulder.

"Fillmore, what are you doing?" Mr. Verde asks sternly.

"Nothing," Tommy answers sullenly, straightening up.

"All right then," says Ms. Johnson. "Danny, maybe you can explain what just happened."

"Not much," Danny replies. "Tommy and I were just having a discussion about the lack of courtesy that he's been showing to Cass here."

Their eyebrows shoot up simultaneously. "OK, Tommy — let's go to my office and you can explain yourself," Mr. Verde commands.

"Danny, you and Cass come with me," Ms. Johnson says. "Let's get this all sorted out."

Tommy slinks away with Mr. Verde, and we head off to Ms. Johnson's office. When we get there, she calls up the video surveillance footage of the hallway, and says, "Before I look at this, why don't you give me your version of what happened?"

"This wasn't Danny's fault!" I blurt out. The last thing I want is Danny being punished for my own stupidity. Instead of getting into it with Tommy, why didn't I tell Mr. Pratt or somebody what was going on? I'm my own worst enemy sometimes, and now Danny might have to pay for it.

"It wasn't your fault, either, Cass," he says. "Tell Ms. Johnson what Tommy's been doing to you."

Between the two of us, we manage to put together the whole story, starting with the party and ending with this morning. Ms. Johnson looks concerned. "Why didn't you report this earlier, Cass? You know we have a zero tolerance bullying policy here. Well, at any rate, let's take a look at this footage and verify that Tommy was the aggressor." We watch, starting from the point where Tommy body checks me into my locker, and sure enough, there's no doubt that Tommy is trying to hurt Danny, who's simply, and very effectively, preventing him from doing that.

"OK," Ms. Johnson says finally. "I think the best thing is for Danny to go home for the rest of the day while we deal with Tommy. Cass, you might as well go too, since your Mom called in for you. She explained about your brother—I'm glad he's all right. I'll see both of you tomorrow."

I'm filled with relief. I never thought I'd say this, but thank God for video surveillance! Danny and I leave the office to go home, and as we pass Mr. Verde's door, we can see that he's going over the same footage as Ms. Johnson. He's saying something to Tommy in a pretty harsh voice, and Tommy is slouched in a chair, staring at the floor and looking unhappy.

Danny offers to walk me home, and I accept gratefully. We talk on the way about Chris, and I bring him up to date. We avoid discussing the fight, until he suddenly stops walking and takes my arm.

"Why didn't you tell me that Tommy was still bothering you?" he asks. "Don't you trust me?"

"Of course I trust you," I protest. "It's just—well—honestly, I didn't want you to hurt him and get in trouble because of me, and now that's happened anyway!" I hang my head and he puts his arms around me.

"Oh, Cass, no it didn't. Just because I know how to fight doesn't mean I'm fool enough to do it outside the ring. I would never have gone after Tommy—he's too stupid and slow. It wouldn't be fair. And I'm not in trouble. You saw the tape—all I'm doing is avoiding getting hit. I've taken enough punches this week, thank you very much! From now on, just trust that I'll always do the right thing, OK?"

"OK," I agree and hug him tight. We start walking again, and I say, "I have to admit, it looked good on Tommy, hitting the ground so hard. He looked stunned, like he couldn't believe it. Talk about embarrassing!"

"I know," Danny laughs. "I think it's safe to say that between you firing your backpack at him, and me taking out his feet, he'll leave both of us alone from now on. You're pretty feisty when you get mad, aren't you?!"

We get to my house just as Mom is arriving with Chris, who jumps out of the car and throws his arms around first me, and next, Danny. Then he charges in the house, presumably to find his Almighty Rat costume. I hope Mom has that talk with him soon about not actually being the Almighty Rat.

Danny smiles after him. "He seems to be over the concussion."

Mom gives Danny a curious look, and he says, "Oh, I was just walking Cass home. I'll be on my way, Mrs. Wilson. I'm glad that Chris is feeling better."

Mom says, "Thanks, Danny. Listen, would you like to come to dinner tonight? I'm sure Cass would be happy to see you later." She smiles innocently at both of us.

"Sure, that would be great—I'll come over around four, if that's all right, then I can hang out with Chris for a while if he's up to it."

We say goodbye, and Mom turns to me. "Will you be OK if I go back to work? You look exhausted. Chris, on the other hand, is a bundle of energy from being cooped up in the hospital, so I doubt if you'll get much rest. The doctor did say that he shouldn't be too active, and definitely no TV or computer, so maybe you can convince him to play some board games."

"Sure that's fine," I reassure her. "Go on—I'll see you later." I give her a list of things to pick up for dinner, since we're having a guest, and she leaves. I stand, staring at the house, willing my tired feet to move, knowing that Chris is in there, raring to go. Then I picture him lying on the floor at Clara's, and suddenly I'm flying through the door calling, "Hey buddy, what game do you want to play first?!"

Chapter 16

D anny arrives at four o'clock on the dot, much to Chris's excitement. I get a minute to ask him what his parents had to say about him being sent home, and he says, "I explained what happened, so they're fine with it. Don't worry, I didn't get into all the details about Tommy harassing you — I just said he was picking on someone and I stepped in."

I laugh. "Well, that's true enough. Why don't you play with Chris while Mom and I are getting dinner ready?"

They go off together to the family room, and Mom and I put together chicken, mashed potatoes, gravy, and veggies. When we call Chris and Danny in, they're laughing their heads off.

"Your brother is a real card shark, Cass," says Danny. "He beat me at every game!" Chris looks extremely pleased with himself, not realizing that Danny most likely let him win.

We're half-way through dinner when Mom says, "So, Cass, I've been thinking about something." I look up at her, and she has a smile on her face, so I know it can't be anything bad. Then again, she was smiling when she first told me about Grant, so...

"What is it?" I ask. Chris and Danny are still eating, Chris talking with his mouth full of mashed potatoes about the Almighty Rat movie, and re-enacting scenes while Danny watches.

"Well, it's occurred to me that you've been doing so much around here these last few years, and you've really given up a lot, and never complained about it. You've done more for your family that most kids your age would have. You deserve something back. So, I think you should take that job at the archaeology camp this summer. I know I said we couldn't afford for you to be away, but we'll make it work somehow. I want you to do this, Cass — it's important."

I'm stunned. I sit there for a moment with my mouth hanging open, but then reality hits me, and I say, "Mom, you know there's no way we can afford to pay someone to look after Chris. Don't worry about me — I like taking care of him. I can always apply next year. Besides, I already told Clara that I'd look after Lindsay too. But thanks, though — I appreciate it, I really do." At this point, I realize that Danny has turned his attention to Mom and me, and he clears his throat.

"Cass, we already talked about this. Didn't you tell your mom that I'm happy to look after Chris and Lindsay while you're gone? And that you didn't have to pay me?"

Mom looks surprised, and I feel myself going red. "Danny, that's wonderful of you to offer — but of course, we'll pay you," Mom says.

"No, I —," I start, then Chris interrupts. "Is Danny going to look after me this summer?! All right!" He pumps his fist in the air, and he and Danny high-five each other, then they both turn to me, beaming.

"See, Cass — Chris is fine with it," says Mom. "And don't worry about the money — I have a feeling that our income might be growing soon," she continues mysteriously.

What could that mean? I wonder. Is she getting a promotion or something? I don't have too long to think about it though, because she turns to Danny and says, "If you're sure it's something you want to do, then we absolutely accept, don't we, Cass?"

All my excuses are ripped away. Chris will be with someone that I know will take good care of him, he's really happy about it, and Mom says we can afford it. I take a deep breath and say, "OK then. I guess I better fill out the application and hand it in right away."

I race upstairs to find it, and bring it and the brochure down to the table. I have it filled in before we get to dessert, and put it in my backpack, ready to give to Mr. Pratt tomorrow. We spend the rest of the meal looking at the brochure and talking about what the camp might be like.

When Danny has to leave, I walk him out to the porch. He says, "You look pretty happy right now."

"I am pretty happy right now," I smile widely. "How can I ever thank you for doing this for me?"

He pulls me close and kisses me. "Just promise me you'll enjoy yourself and not worry about the kids. They're in good hands," he says.

"I know," I reply and hug him tight.

After he's gone, I sit on the porch for a while, thinking about how things seem to be working out. I can't believe it—this might actually happen. I just hope I'm not too late; I vow to myself that Mr. Pratt's office will be my first stop tomorrow.

Next morning, I get up and out of the house as fast as I can, to make sure I see Mr. Pratt before classes start. My heart is racing—what if all the positions are filled already? What will I do then? My feet fly along the pavement, and before I know it, I'm sitting in the outer guidance office waiting for Mr. Pratt, tapping my fingers impatiently. He walks through the door, and I barely give him time to put down his briefcase and unlock his office before I'm right behind him, application out.

"Oh, Cass!" he exclaims. "What brings you here so early in the morning? Is everything all right?"

"Everything's fine," I reply, holding out the application and waving it at him. "I brought this for you. I'm not too late, am I?" Please don't say yes, I beg silently.

"What day is it? Wednesday? Oh, I think it's fine — I'll fax this over to the university right away this morning, and call Professor McGarry to make sure he gets it. You certainly waited until the last minute!"

He takes the application out of my hand, and I have an overwhelming urge to hug him, but I don't, mainly because I think it would embarrass him more than me. He tells me that Professor McGarry should let me know very soon, since summer's not too far off. I walk down the hall, floating on air, until I realize that people are whispering and giving me looks as I go by. It's making me really uncomfortable, so I duck into the bathroom to wait for the halls to clear a little. While I'm waiting, in walks Jasmine Ogilvy, Miss Popularity herself. I go to the sink and start washing my hands. She comes over and stands beside me. God, is she going to tell me off about Tommy? As far as I know, they hang out with the same group of friends.

"Hi," she says. This is actually the first time we've ever spoken. She doesn't seem threatening — I wonder what she wants?

"Hi," I answer, reaching for the paper towels. I look at her with curiosity. She's really pretty, almost model-beautiful — I can see why Sam, my lesbian cafeteria friend, has a crush on her.

As I'm drying my hands, she says quietly, "I just wanted to say thanks."

"Thanks for what?" I ask. What on earth is she thanking me for? Not taking her place as Prom Queen? I stare at her and wait.

"For doing what you did to Tommy, you know, standing up to him. He treated me the same way last year when I wouldn't go to Lakewood Park with him." Lakewood Park is the place people go when they want to be 'alone' with each other. She looks like she's going to cry. "He started calling me names, telling people that I was a slut behind my back, posting rumours about me online, and pretty soon, I lost most of my friends. Once, he even pushed me into my locker, just like he did to you yesterday. But I never had the guts to tell him off, let alone hit him with my backpack. Maybe if I had, he wouldn't have done it to you, and all the other girls he's made miserable."

A tear rolls down her face, and she wipes it away delicately. I'm not sure what to say, considering I barely know her, but I put my hand on her shoulder and tell her, "Tommy's a snake. I let it go on way too long — don't blame yourself. We all let him get away with too much, but now everyone knows what kind of jerk he is. And by the way, anyone who would stop being your friend because of Tommy's stupid rumours wasn't worth having as a friend in the first place."

She nods, and another tear escapes. "I know. Things are much better now — and I have university to look forward to for next year — no more high school drama, right?"

"You're lucky you get to escape. I still have one more year to go."

"You'll get through it just fine," she says. "I hear you have a really great boyfriend. And you don't have to worry about Tommy for a while — he's been suspended indefinitely. There's a line-up of girls outside Mr. Verde's office just waiting to file complaints about him. I've already talked to Mr. Verde myself — first thing this morning."

We part ways, and I head out to look for Danny. I find him waiting by my locker, and I tell him about my encounter with Jasmine. He shakes his head in disbelief. "I knew the guy was a loser, but I had no idea how much of a loser he was."

As we're heading to class, I notice Tara Connelly and Megan Pearson staring at us as we go by. "Hang on a minute," I say to Danny. "Wait here—I'll be right back." I'm fed up with these two gossipy idiots and decide to put an end to whatever they're up to—after Tommy, this should be a piece of cake. I stop right in front of them, and say, "What are you staring at?"

Tara's eyes go wide and she says breathlessly, "I heard about what happened yesterday with Tommy. I always thought he was so nice!"

Megan turns to her and says, "You should have seen Danny—it was so amazing the way he took Tommy down. I told you he was hot!"

"I know!" Tara replies, giggling.

"You're so lucky, Cass!" Megan giggles back, and I think, God, these two are unbelievable.

"Well, anyway," I say, dumbfounded by their flakiness. "See you in English class."

"See you!" they both chirp happily after me.

"What was that all about?" Danny asks as we continue down the hall together. "Those two girls are so weird."

"You'll be happy to know that they think you're 'hot'," I tell him, and he laughs his head off.

Chapter 17

I arrive home after school, relieved that today wasn't as bad as I thought it might be. With Tommy out of the picture for who-knows-how-long, and everyone thinking both Danny and I are heroes for showing him up, it was actually pretty good. People are so fickle, though—the same kids who were laughing at Tommy's stupid jokes last week are the same people who are calling him a creep this week. Well, at least the truth is out.

Chris comes through the door full of excitement. All his friends know that he was in the hospital, and today he got to tell them the story of Karate Chris and the Psycho. He's a bit of a hero too, and definitely proud of himself. Mom talked to him last night about the difference between cartoons and reality. He said he knew that, but he couldn't stand by and watch someone hurt his sister, that he did the only thing he knew how to do to protect me. Mom promised to enrol him in a proper karate class in the fall, although where she's getting the money for that is also a mystery.

I'm in the kitchen, starting to get dinner ready, when the phone rings. Probably Mom, wondering if I need her to pick up anything. I answer the phone, and a man's voice says, "Can I speak to Cassandra Wilson, please?"

My heart jumps, and I reply, "Speaking."

"Hi there," he says. "My name is Professor Mc-Garry. I received your application to be a counsellor at the archaeology camp I run during the summer. I'm just calling to offer you a position, if you're interested."

Interested?! Is he kidding? I blurt out, "Yes, very much, I'd love the job!" My hands are shaking as I write down the date and time of an information meeting that I need to attend.

"I look forward to meeting you then," he finishes. "Your guidance counsellor is a friend of mine and he's spoken very highly of you."

Good old Mr. Pratt! He really is dedicated to his students. I can't wait to tell Mom the good news — and Danny too, of course. I'm just about to text Danny, when Mom comes walking in.

"Hey, you're home early," I say excitedly. "Guess what?!"

"What?" she laughs. "You seem pretty happy about something."

I tell her about the phone call and we both whoop and hug each other. Then she says, "Actually, I'm home because I have some big news too!"

"What?!" I ask. "Did you get a promotion?" Maybe this is what she's been so secretive about — the extra money will come in handy, that's for sure. Then, I notice something sparkling on her finger, and my heart skips a beat.

"No, even better!" she answers, waggling the ring in front of my face. "Look!"

"Oh, Mom, wow," I say, trying to keep the disappointment out of my voice. "An engagement ring — that's just fantastic." I don't mean it — I mean, I'm happy for her, but this is what I've been dreading. Once again, I picture good old Grant, sitting in Dad's chair at the dinner table, asking us about our days, and I feel myself start to tear up.

"Oh, Cass, what's the matter? You're happy for me, aren't you?" She looks concerned and worried.

"Of course," I sniff. "It's just—" I start to cry in earnest. I feel so stupid, ruining her moment like this, but I can't help it. She pulls me out of the kitchen and over to the couch, where we sit down together.

"Honey, is it because of your Dad?" she asks. I nod. "But Cass, he would be happy for me. He wanted us to move on, not mourn for him forever!"

"I know," I sob. "I just really miss him, and the thought of you marrying someone else means that he's really gone!" I've never told her any of this before, how sometimes I pretended that he wasn't really dead, that he was just at work, and he'd walk in the door any minute and be back with us. I tell her now, in a jumble of words and tears, and she hugs me close.

"Sweetheart, I'm sorry you've been so sad about this for so long. I only wish you'd told me ages ago. I spent years feeling the same way, you know. Like any moment, I'd hear his laugh, and I'd look out the window, and there he'd be mowing the lawn, or digging in the sandbox with you. It wasn't until I met Grant that I realized that was never going to happen. I had to move on. Your Dad would understand. And Grant knows that he can never take the place of your Dad—he's happy just to be a member of our family." Then she starts to cry too, and we hug again.

Finally, we both collect ourselves, and I say, "I used to love playing with him in that sandbox. I think that's what inspired me to think about archaeology.

"I know," she says. "Remember the time capsule you two buried when you were five? You were so excited about it!"

"Time capsule?" I ask wonderingly. "Where?"

"In the sandbox, of course. You spent two days finding just the right things to go into it, don't you remember? Your dad put some things in it too. I can't believe I'd forgotten about it until just now. It should still be there—we should go dig it up!"

"You mean, now? Can we?!" I'm thrilled at the thought that there might be something there. I honestly don't remember what could be in it, but I can't wait to find out.

"Of course, if you want to—let's grab some shovels!"

With that, we head out. Chris joins us, clamouring to know what we're up to. I hand him a shovel and tell him to dig a hole as far down as he can. It couldn't be buried very deep, just deep enough to be beyond the reach of regular playtime digging. We work away for a while in silence, randomly choosing spots and digging down, when suddenly my shovel hits something solid.

"I think I found it!" I call out. Mom and Chris put their shovels down and come over to see. I bend down and start scratching dirt away with my fingers. It's not long before the outline of a box becomes visible.

"What is it?" Chris asks in wonderment. I just stare at the box, imagining what treasures it might hold, then I pull it out of its hole.

"It's a time capsule, honey," Mom says to Chris quietly. "Cass and your Dad buried it when she was a little girl."

"What's in it?" he asks.

I look up. "I don't remember," I say. "Do you want to find out?"

He nods his head enthusiastically, and I carry the box carefully back into the house, putting it down gently on the kitchen table, which Mom has quickly covered with newspapers. The box itself is quite ordinary, a plain, square aluminum tin with a tight lid. The words "Do Not Open For 10 Years!" are scuffed but still faintly visible, written in permanent marker. I try to pry off the lid with my fingers, but it's rusted tight.

Mom says, "Hang on." She rummages in the junk drawer and pulls out a screwdriver. "Try prying it with this," she suggests. I take the screwdriver and do as she says. The lid starts to lift up with a scraping sound. When it's high enough up, I grab the edge, pull, and the whole thing comes off. Inside the box are two large sealed jars, one labelled 'Cass' in childish printing, and the other labelled 'Dad' in more mature writing.

"Open them, open them!" Chris explodes with excitement. Mom laughs and says, "Give her a minute, Chris." She and I both seem to realize that this is an important moment, as if what's in the jars could have a tremendous impact on both of us.

I pick up the "Cass" jar; the lid is tight but it begins to turn with a little effort. Once the lid is completely off, I tip the jar so that its contents spill out onto the newspaper. What an assortment of odds and ends! A tiny doll, a spoon, a crayon drawing of what looks like Dad and me digging in the sandbox, a seashell, a rock, and three pipe cleaners, blue, red, and yellow, twisted around each other. Chris fingers each item carefully, and says, "What are all these for?"

"I don't know," I admit. "Just things that I liked when I was little, I guess."

"Open the other jar now," he demands impatiently. I ruffle his hair, and then start unscrewing the second lid. I hesitate and look at Mom, who nods encouragingly.

I go to pull out the first item and then my breath is gone as I begin to realize that this is my Dad, these are the last things I'll ever get from him, all I have left of him, and that when he put these things in this jar, he had no idea that I would be opening it without him. I'm suddenly afraid, for some reason, and my hands start to shake.

"Come on, Cass—let's see!" Chris appeals. I steel myself and take out the first item, a folded piece of paper. I open it slowly; it's another cartoon drawing of Dad and me digging in the sandbox, this one done by him.

Mom says, "I remember those pictures now. You both did one, and I had to judge whose was better. I declared it a tie—I didn't want any hurt feelings!" We all smile, and Chris says, "What else is in there?"

I pull out the next thing, a souvenir pen from the zoo. "Look!" exclaims Chris. "I have one like that, too! You took me there last year, Mom, remember?" She nods, and I think back to my trip with Mom and Dad to the local zoo. All I really remember is Dad having a great time teasing the monkeys, and ending the day with pizza and ice cream. But I guess it must have meant a lot to Dad, since he put the pen in there. Then I take out the final treasure, another piece of folded paper, this one lined.

"What's that?" Chris wants to know immediately.

I unfold it and stare at it. "It's a letter," I breathe.

Mom says to Chris, "Let's give Cass a minute alone to read her letter, OK?" He looks at me, then back at her, and seems to understand the seriousness of her request. "I'll be in the family room if you need me," she says.

I nod and wait until they leave before I open the letter fully. It's written in his careful printing, a little faded but still legible. I start to read:

Hi Cass!

So today's the day we open our time capsule! I know 10 years sounded like forever when you were little, but time really does go by quickly and you've always been a patient girl. I'll bet your smile is as beautiful now as it was on the day we buried our jars. I can't wait to give you a hug after you read this. Know that I'll always be here for you no matter what, and that I'll always love you.

Daddy

A tear falls down my cheek and lands on the paper. I wipe it off, fold the letter quickly back up, and put it in my pocket. It's hard to imagine that he had no idea that when I read it, he would already have been dead for 5 years. I'd give anything for a hug from him now, but that will never happen again—I just have to come to terms with that. Mom's been able to move on, although it took her a while; maybe it's time for me to let her do it without making her feel guilty. Somehow, these last words coming from him after so long are a comfort instead of reminding me of his loss. He always did love me, and I'm sure that, wherever he is now, he still does. And Mom deserves to be happy after so many years of missing him. I dry my eyes, and carefully put the jars back into the tin, then clear off the table. Mom hears the noise and comes into the kitchen, looking at me for a sign.

"I'm OK," I tell her. "Look, it's been a rough couple of weeks, but I just want you to know that I'm really happy that you and Grant are getting married. Honest. I think we should celebrate—why don't you call him and ask him to come over for dinner?"

"Really?" she says. "That would be wonderful. I have an even better idea—why don't you call Danny and see if he'd like to join us? That way we can celebrate your good news too!"

Danny is thrilled for me and agrees to come over right away. Grant is really pleased about the invitation and offers to bring take-out and a bottle of champagne. "The classiest kind of dinner," he kids.

As we're enjoying our impromptu celebration, Chris asks, through a mouthful of French fries, "What was in your letter?"

"What letter?" Danny looks at me quizzically.

"Oh, I'll tell you about it later," I say. "Can someone pass the salt, please?"

"Right-o," Grant says cheerfully, handing me the salt and giving me a mock-salute. I stop short—my Dad used to do the exact same thing. But somehow, it feels all right. I understand that it's not Grant taking Dad's place, but that he's just a great guy who's a lot like my Dad. As I look around the table at Mom's beaming face, at Danny and Chris laughing at each other, at Grant looking so happy to be a part of everything, I realize that, with these people, in this moment, I finally know who I am. And I smile.